THE SPOTTED DOG LAST SEEN

THE SPOTTED DOG
LAST SEEN

JESSICA SCOTT KERRIN

leaving
nodded
clapped
genuinely
haunting
attack
slipping
twinkly

Groundwood Books / House of Anansi Press
Toronto Berkeley

Groundwood Books / House of Anansi Press
110 Spadina Avenue, Suite 801, Toronto, Ontario M5V 2K4
or c/o Publishers Group West
1700 Fourth Street, Berkeley, CA 94710

We acknowledge for their financial support of our publishing program the
Canada Council for the Arts, the Government of Canada through the Canada
Book Fund (CBF) and the Ontario Arts Council.

 Canada Council   Conseil des Arts
for the Arts   du Canada

 ONTARIO ARTS COUNCIL
CONSEIL DES ARTS DE L'ONTARIO

Library and Archives Canada Cataloguing in Publication
Kerrin, Jessica Scott
The spotted dog last seen / written by Jessica Scott Kerrin.
Also issued in electronic format.
ISBN 978-1-55498-387-2 (bound).—ISBN 978-1-55498-401-5 (pbk.)
I. Title.
PS8621.E77S66 2013   jC813'.6   C2013-900398-3

Cover illustration by Sam Kalda
Design by Michael Solomon

Groundwood Books is committed to protecting our natural environment.
As part of our efforts, the interior of this book is printed on paper that contains
100% post-consumer recycled fibers, is acid-free and is processed chlorine-free.
Printed and bound in Canada

FSC
www.fsc.org
MIX
Paper from
responsible sources
FSC® C016245

FOR the little boy who lost his little brother

Table of Contents

Prologue

THIS IS A LARGE cemetery for such a small town. And old. You told us once that some of the gravestones date back hundreds of years. But I didn't make a habit of hanging out in cemeteries when you were doing the telling. Believe me, I'd rather have been anywhere else.

Did you know I arrived alone that first day? Pascal Bender and Merrilee Takahashi were supposed to meet me at one o'clock by the iron gate. There I stood. It was three minutes past one. And then it started to rain.

The first raindrops plopped against the grave markers, which teetered this way and that over the lumpy ground. I was sure that even a ghost could knock down some of them, just by floating past at sunset.

Sorry. I know how you felt about ghosts.

And vampires. And zombies.

I could see that there were different types of stones — brown, white, bluish gray — but I didn't know which was which.

And all those carved symbols on the stones? Well, the angels were easy to spot. Their wings were a dead giveaway. But I didn't know what the other symbols meant, like the ones with clasping hands or a baby lamb. And all those skulls and crossbones? I was sure that meant the cemetery was full of dead pirates!

When Pascal and Merrilee didn't show up, I thought I must be waiting in the wrong section. I was standing in the oldest part of the cemetery, where the stones were covered in lichen and eroded words. Maybe we were supposed to start in the newer section and work our way backwards through time.

But I didn't know where the newer part of the cemetery might be. I certainly didn't know who would be buried there.

You.

One

Reading
Weathered Marble

WIND HOWLED through the trees that surrounded me. Boughs overhead moaned. The roots beneath my feet wrapped tightly around the buried coffins to hold the trees to the ground.

And all the while, I stood at the cemetery gate trying my best to ignore the posted warning signs:

Beware of Falling Gravestones
Enter at Your Own Risk
Closed at Sunset
No Dogs Allowed

Just who did the gate think it was fooling? Sure, it looked secure enough, but when it was locked at night, the gate would be useless at keeping anything inside that wanted to get out.

And I wasn't worried about the living.

Then I heard a shrill four-fingered whistle across the street from the cemetery.

"Derek!" the whistler hollered from the front steps of the old stone library that had once been a church. "We're in here!"

I grabbed my knapsack and bolted from the cemetery gate, cold heebie-jeebies charging down my spine. But when I got to the crosswalk, I stopped in my tracks.

I looked left, right, left, and then left, right, left again before taking a careful step off the curb. The extra checking was a safety habit that I couldn't seem to shake, not even when fleeing a spooky graveyard in the cold rain. After crossing the street, I scrambled up the granite steps to the library with relief.

I'd never been to this library before. Even though it was no longer a church, its stained-glass windows had been saved. Each one was filled with scenes of people in robes and sandals — the men with beards, the women's heads covered by hoods, many of them weeping or looking up to the sky with their hands clasped, some on their knees, heads bowed, beams of light shining down.

"You must be Derek. I'm Loyola Louden."

Loyola was basketball-player tall compared to my own husky self. If you asked me what my favorite subject at school was, I would not say, "Gym." But I was guessing that Loyola sure would. She effortlessly held a large stack of books with one hand as she shook my hand with her other gigantic one. At least she didn't squeeze hard. I really hated that.

"Do you supervise cemetery duty?" I asked.

"No. I'm a university student," Loyola said. "I work here part-time."

"I'm supposed to report for cemetery duty by the gate," I explained.

"The Twillingate Cemetery Brigade gives lessons here whenever it's raining."

"Lessons?" I repeated with alarm. I thought cemetery duty was supposed to be dead easy, like picking up litter or planting flowers around that ugly towering gate or straightening gravestones that looked like they were about to topple over.

She ignored my unease and led me inside, past stacks and stacks of books, to the research area where Pascal and Merrilee sat waiting.

"Hey," I said to them without much enthusiasm.

Merrilee answered by pushing her glasses higher on her nose. Pascal gave me a tight nod. They looked about as glum as I felt about our new school assignment.

Queensview Elementary has been getting grade-six students to do community service work during the last three months of the school year for as long as anyone can remember. Usually, everyone gets to pick from a list of places that need volunteers. Soup kitchens. Homeless shelters. Seniors' residences. That kind of thing.

I thought the seniors would be okay. I'd sit around

playing cards with them and whatnot. Talk about whatever war was going on. How hard could that be?

But I was sick at home the day we made our selections. Not really sick, I just had an eye infection. Pink eye is what they call it. Supposed to be highly spreadable. By the time I got back to school, all that was left was cemetery duty.

"Do you want me to call your teacher?" my mom had blurted as soon she found out. "See if someone will switch with you?"

"No one's dying to go to the cemetery," I had said, which is pretty funny, now that I think about it. "And anyway, I'll be fine."

She had turned away, but not before I saw her frown.

"I'll be fine," I had repeated, trying to convince myself more than her.

I slid into the empty seat beside Pascal. I was not used to seeing him out of school uniform, or Merrilee for that matter, although I spotted her familiar red plastic jacket with the bunnies-and-carrots print draped over her chair. I hoped they would notice my t-shirt. It read, *Change is good. You go first.*

I like to collect sayings I've heard and print the best ones on t-shirts. Lately, I had been giving them away as gifts. My dad got, *I'm fine*, with a bloodstain printed beneath the words. He likes to wear it in his workshop in the garage or when he goes to the hardware store.

I thought that if I were to make a t-shirt for Pascal,

it might read, *There are three kinds of people: those who are good at math and those who aren't.* Pascal had an answer for everything, even if he had to take a wild stab in the dark.

But I wasn't so sure about Merrilee. I didn't know her as well as Pascal, although I remembered that she was quite the archaeologist when she was little. She had a peculiar habit of burying things in the school's sandbox, then later digging them up. Maybe her t-shirt would read, *X marks the spot.*

The cemetery work crew we were assigned to arrived in full force — all three of them.

"Students, I'd like you to meet the Twillingate Cemetery Brigade. This is Mr. Creelman, Mr. Preeble and Mr. Wooster," Loyola announced.

Each one glowered more fiercely than the next. All three stood dripping in their raincoats. Loyola eyed the stack of books that Merrilee had been leafing through and quietly moved them to another table for protection.

Creelman broke away from the trio. His thick white eyebrows reminded me of a portrait of my grandfather that I'd done back in grade one. I had been really inventive by gluing on cotton balls for his eyebrows.

"No sense cleaning grave markers today," he announced, digging out a thick wad of wrinkled yellowed notes from inside his raincoat pocket. "Instead, you'll have your first lesson on how to read weathered stones."

Creelman paused. Was he expecting us to clap? All he got was the sound of rain slamming against the cheerless stained glass above our heads.

"Let's see how much you know," Creelman said, plowing along even without applause. "What are most of our nineteenth-century stones made out of?"

"Nineteenth century," Pascal repeated. "You mean the really old ones?"

"Not old! Weathered!" Creelman barked, pounding the table for effect.

I startled. Merrilee flinched.

"Concrete?" Pascal guessed undaunted.

As I said, he had an answer for everything, but even I knew that he was way, way off.

Creelman stared him down, probably trying to figure out if Pascal was joking or not. His cotton-ball eyebrows collided into one straight line.

"Anybody else?" he growled, turning to Merrilee and me.

We quickly shook our heads, me unable to look away from those comical brows.

"Marble," he pronounced. And then he repeated himself as if we were idiots. "Mar-ble."

We shifted in our hard wooden seats.

"Does marble last forever?" he asked, eyebrows now arched.

It felt like a trick question. Merrilee and I didn't bite, but Pascal quickly weighed in.

"Yes, it does. For sure. Look at the ancient Greek statues."

Creelman snorted.

"Ancient Greek statues aren't forever!" he declared, pounding the table again. "That's why there aren't many left and they end up inside museums for protection!"

He had a point. It even silenced Pascal for a moment.

"And do you know why marble doesn't last?" Creelman continued, laying another trap.

I looked around for help. Preeble and Wooster were standing off to the side appearing smug, as if they knew the answers but weren't about to share. Loyola was gone. I spotted her back at the front desk helping a daycare group sign out picture books.

"Sulfur dioxide," Creelman declared, but he didn't pound the table. Instead, he stood with his arms crossed, giving us plenty of time for this fact to sink in.

I wondered if my mom should make the call about cemetery duty after all.

"And where does sulfur dioxide come from?" Creelman demanded.

He was relentless!

Desperately, I looked over to Loyola, who had finished checking out the books. I caught her eye, but then she quickly busied herself by sharpening pencils. She was not coming back any time soon. Traitor!

"The periodic table?" Pascal guessed.

The periodic table? I was tempted to inch my chair

closer to Merrilee so that Pascal had plenty of room to dig his own grave. Good grief!

"Burning coal power!" Creelman replied, his eyes widening.

Even though we knew it was coming, all three of us jumped when he pounded the table yet again.

"Sulfur dioxide is the enemy of gravestones," Creelman continued, as if he were talking about some new plague or a campfire ghost story. "It steals letters and makes our grave markers unreadable."

Pollution. Got it. I sneaked a peek at the wall clock. This was going to be a very long afternoon. I almost wished I was back in the cemetery, despite the rain.

Almost.

"Part of your job will be to read and record our gravestones so that the information doesn't disappear," he leaned in, "*forever*."

As if rehearsed, Preeble pulled a small mirror from the pocket of his raincoat, handed it to Creelman, then took a precise step back beside Wooster. Creelman moved beneath the nearest stained-glass window and held the mirror in front of the engraved plaque mounted in the shadow of the windowsill.

"If there's plenty of light, like in this library, you can use a mirror. You hold it over the gravestone like this," explained Creelman, flashing the mirror across the plaque, "and redirect the light at an angle so that the carved words are highlighted in shadows. See?"

The words etched on the plaque really popped out. It read, *Restored by the Twillingate Cemetery Brigade*.

Despite the table pounding, I was a little impressed.

"But sometimes there's not much light," Creelman said, his eyebrows casting a shadow, his face clouding over.

That was Wooster's cue to pull out a paintbrush from his pocket and hand it to Creelman, then return to his spot beside Preeble.

"What you do is take a brush and some plain water." Creelman demonstrated by brushing the air. "When you wet the surface, you move the dirt into the carved letters and lighten the surrounding surface at the same time. Then it's easier to read."

Makes sense, I thought. It was simple to follow now that the table pounding had stopped.

Creelman began to lay out his yellowed sheets of paper in front of us.

"Even with all that, you'll still need to become an expert at deciphering engraved characters that have partially disappeared. Have a look."

The three of us leaned in. Creelman's papers contained charts of what carved numbers looked like after they had weathered for one hundred years and then two hundred years.

"I need someone to demonstrate," Creelman said. He slowly scanned the three of us, and his eyes landed on me.

"Okay," I croaked, having very little choice.

He handed me a nubby pencil.

"Write the numbers 1 through 9 on this piece of paper," he instructed.

I did.

"Now look. See how all your strokes are even?"

Everyone inspected my numbers. I have to admit that I do write neatly. My notebook where I record my collection of t-shirt sayings is a thing of beauty.

"But it isn't so with numbers hand-carved in marble. They are carved by uneven chisel strokes. Take the number 4. The carver has to lean in hard to make one long downward stroke, and then finish the rest of the number with short light taps. Over time, those little strokes fade away, leaving only the deep downward stroke, until finally you can't tell a 1 from a 4."

"How do we figure out which is which?" Pascal asked.

"Good question!" Creelman replied, not scowling for the first time that afternoon. "Your only clue is the spacing. Look here. The downward strokes in the year 1811 are spaced more evenly than the year 1814."

Even Merrilee nodded in interest.

"The numbers 2, 3 and 5 are in the next group. Over time, only the deep curve on the right side of all three numbers remains — here at the top of the 2, here at the bottom of the 5 and here, twice for the number 3."

By now, I'd completely forgotten about the cemetery. As we studied Creelman's charts, I began to feel as if we were training to become detectives for hidden codes.

"Next are the numbers 6, 9 and 0. They also have deep curves on both sides that remain over time. The number 6 will have a long curve on the left and a short curve on the right. Nine is just the opposite. And see here? Zero will have two long curves."

Look at that, I thought, taking in the lesson.

"Last are the numbers 7 and 8. When carvers engrave an 8, they have to cut a deep diagonal line in the middle that is the last to fade away. But unlike the number 8, the number 7 has a long deep diagonal cut that runs all the way to the bottom."

Then, just when I was not expecting it, Creelman pounded the table and declared, "Sevens never die!"

From the safety of her desk, Loyola Louden looked our way with a startle.

The lights flickered overhead.

"Now, we're going to leave you to study these charts. When we get back, there'll be a quiz. We can't have you making any errors when you're recording our gravestones."

With that, Creelman, Preeble and Wooster marched past the book stacks and out the front door, leaving behind the yellowed sheets, a mirror and three puddles on the marble floor.

Rain smashed against the stained glass. The only things missing were a mighty flash of lightning, a full-on power failure and sinister violin music.

"What was *that* about?" Merrilee demanded. She shoved the yellowed papers away and reached over to grab one of the books from the pile that Loyola had moved to the next table.

"You're not going to study?" I asked.

Although I was not the best student at school, I did study, especially when I knew there'd be a quiz. And I still kind of liked it when my mom posted my better efforts on the fridge door. I think she had even saved the portrait of my grandfather. She said it was a keeper.

Merrilee gave me a withering look.

But that didn't bother me nearly as much as the table pounding that was sure to come if I failed the quiz, so I got to work. Pascal studied the sheets, too. Then we took turns writing out eroded dates and seeing if the other could guess the correct numbers.

Eventually, Loyola returned to our table to chat. She noisily scraped a chair across the marble floor and sat down.

"So, what do you think of the donation?" she asked Merrilee.

"Looks pretty good," Merrilee said, leafing through a book. "I'd like to sign it out."

I stopped quizzing Pascal. "What donation?" I asked.

"Several copies of the book Merrilee has arrived by mail this morning. There's no return address, no way to find out who the donor is."

I leaned over to read the cover of Merrilee's book. *The Purloined Parrot.*

"What does *purloined* mean?" I asked.

"Stolen," Merrilee said.

I shrugged. The book still sounded pretty girly.

"How's it going here?" Loyola asked brightly, despite the surrounding gloom.

"Okay," I said, tidying up Creelman's papers of eroded numbers. "But what's with all the table pounding and whatnot?"

"Mr. Creelman's dead serious about the cemetery," Loyola said, grinning at her choice of words. "He's a founding member of the Twillingate Cemetery Brigade."

"Are they ever coming back?" Pascal asked, leaning into the central aisle for a better view of the front door.

"Oh, sure," Loyola replied. "Mr. Preeble and Mr. Wooster are probably finishing up at the cafe down the street by now, and Mr. Creelman is likely pacing the shop's back alley, trying not to smoke."

"He smokes?" I repeated.

"Poor guy," Loyola said. "He told me that he wants to quit for good just once before he dies."

There was a commotion at the door, and we craned our necks to watch the arrival of the Brigade. They made a beeline for our table while Loyola returned to the front desk, pushing a squeaky trolley of books along the way.

"Ready for your quiz?" Creelman demanded, his two cronies on standby.

"You're dripping," Merrilee said kindly. "Let me get you some paper towels."

She got up from the table with the slightest grin.

She didn't fool me. I knew exactly what she was doing. She was getting out of the quiz, that's what she was doing, and she was going to take her sweet time finding those paper towels.

From his pocket, Creelman dug out a stack of cue cards wrapped in a thick elastic band, each with an eroded date on it. And that's how it went — him holding up a card and us calling out the year. Merrilee took forever to return, and sure enough, by then, we were done.

Creelman scooped up his yellowed papers from the table.

"See you next Wednesday. Thirteen hundred hours sharp."

"Thirteen hundred hours? I thought we were only volunteering on Wednesdays for the next three months," Pascal said. "Just until we graduate."

Creelman shot him a sober look before leading the Brigade away without a word.

I lingered until they were gone, and then I explained military time to Pascal. We packed up our knapsacks to go.

Outside, it poured. I stood on the steps to zip my

coat while Pascal took off in the direction of his home. Merrilee remained behind to sign out her book. I looked across the street at the cemetery, glad to have avoided my duties in there, at least for now.

Lightning flashed.

Thunder clapped.

Darkness descended.

I half expected to hear an evil laugh coming from the other side of the looming iron gate.

"Well," I half joked to myself out loud. "This certainly has all the makings of a horror movie."

Two

———

Gravestone Carvings

I PUSHED DARK thoughts about cemetery duty away until the next Wednesday. I hoped it would be raining hard again so that we could have another lesson in the safety of the library. Instead, I woke up to a blue-sky day.

Instant dread.

"How'd you sleep?" my mom chirped, her standard question at breakfast.

But I could hear an edge in her voice. She knew it was Wednesday, too.

"Good," I lied.

She looked at me just a little too long.

I didn't feel like telling her that I had had a nightmare last night. The same one I had had for months and months when I was little, always waking up screaming in a cold sweat.

The one with the orange rubber ball.

I had not had *that* nightmare in years. I had almost

forgotten about it. Perhaps this was just a random glitch, and things would go back to normal. Yes, that was it.

I dug into my cereal, even though I didn't feel like eating. The flakes somehow tasted like wrinkled yellowed paper.

Back upstairs, I took deep breaths. Then I got dressed and put on my t-shirt that read, *If the sky's the limit, why are there footprints on the moon?*

Pascal and Merrilee were waiting inside the iron gate when I arrived that afternoon. It was warm, but Merrilee still had on her red plastic bunnies-and-carrots jacket.

"Where's the Brigade?" I asked.

"At the library," Pascal said.

"So we're back in the library?" I asked. I practically whooped as I took an eager step in that direction.

"No. They told us to wait here."

I stopped dead in my tracks.

"Oh."

I reluctantly rejoined the group.

"Why'd you sign up for cemetery duty?" Pascal asked. "You don't seem the type."

"I didn't," I said. "I had pink eye. The cemetery was all that was left."

Pascal nodded sympathetically.

"Dentist appointment," he said, pointing to himself and shrugging.

"What about you, Merrilee?" I asked. "Were you sick, too?"

"No," she said matter-of-factly. "This was my first choice."

First choice! We looked at her as if she might turn into a werewolf or a vampire at that exact moment. She fiddled with the drawstrings of her hood, in no hurry to give us further explanation. We kept staring.

Dead silence.

Finally, she muttered, "I like to be outside."

So do werewolves and vampires, I thought warily. Especially in cemeteries.

"Here they come," Pascal warned, looking past my shoulder.

I turned. Creelman, Preeble and Wooster were making their way along the sidewalk at a surprisingly brisk pace. They had just crossed the street from the library. Loyola Louden stood on the steps to wave them off, then disappeared back inside.

"Uh-oh," Pascal said. "Looks like we're in for another lesson."

Each member of the Brigade was carrying a small stack of books. Pascal and I groaned.

Creelman greeted us, eyeing my t-shirt, but choosing to ignore it.

"Good afternoon," he said, almost like a challenge.

I wondered if Preeble and Wooster ever spoke.

We mumbled some polite words in reply.

"So, which headstones are we tackling today?" Pascal asked, boldly ignoring the books.

He stood with his hands on his hips while surveying the vast selection of skulls and crossbones before him.

"Tackling?" Creelman snapped. "That's not how it works. You need to know about what you're tackling first before you learn how to tackle it. Today's lesson is symbolism."

Pascal dropped his hands to his sides and tilted his head with a confused look.

"Sym-bol-ism," Creelman repeated syllable by syllable, as if dealing with preschoolers.

He thrust his stack of books at me. Preeble and Wooster handed theirs over to Pascal and Merrilee.

"We want you to make your way around this part of the cemetery, from the gate to that first hedgerow. Study all the carvings, and if you don't know what a symbol means, look it up."

"A symbol," Pascal said pensively. "Is that the same as a simile?"

"A what now?" Creelman asked, sticking out his lower jaw.

"He's confusing his terms," Merrilee said. She turned to Pascal. "A *symbol* is a thing that stands for something else. A *simile* is a figure of speech comparing two completely different things."

"What's the difference?" Pascal asked.

I jumped in, having included a few similes in my collection of t-shirt sayings.

"A tree in a graveyard is a simile if I say that the tree stood alone like a pirate on trial for looting. But a skull and crossbones is a symbol for pirates because it means danger."

I looked at Creelman, pretty pleased with myself.

"You think a skull and crossbones is a symbol for pirates? Not here, it isn't," he barked. He pointed to my stack of books and jabbed three times at the cover of the top one. "Look. It. Up. We'll be back in an hour. There will be a quiz."

It sounded like a threat.

Creelman turned on his heel and marched away, with Preeble and Wooster following in tight formation. I thought I heard him grumble something about pirates.

I checked out my stack of books. They had deadly boring titles, such as *Grave Matters*, *Final Destination* and *Eternal Landscapes*. Each was filled with grainy black-and-white photographs of grave markers, a sea of gray when I flipped through the pages in fast motion.

I couldn't believe it. The school's sign-up sheet for cemetery duty had promised that "volunteers would be in for a charming and delightful romp through the ages."

Hilarious.

I looked around. Merrilee was already wandering among the teetering stones, having abandoned her pile of books on top of a gravestone that had fallen face first to the ground. Pascal had moved to a nearby marker, flashing sunlight across the carved numbers with a mirror that he had pocketed.

"Is it working?" I asked, remembering last week's lesson.

"Yes! Look!" he exclaimed.

The numbers magically popped out from the shadows.

I was about to call Merrilee in my excitement, but by then she was too far away, floating from stone to stone like a butterfly in a meadow.

"I'm going to start over there," I announced to Pascal, feeling the need to report in to someone. I pointed to a particularly old section with plenty of lichen on stones that stood bunched together in small family groupings, all facing the same direction.

Pascal barely glanced at me as he moved to another stone with his mirror, leaving his pile of books beside Merrilee's.

I headed out on my own. Really, I had no choice. There was that threatened quiz, after all. But I was actually glad to look up symbols. It would keep my mind off things. I just had to make sure that I didn't wander too far away from the cemetery gate, in case I needed a quick escape route.

First things first. What were all those skulls and crossbones about? I flipped through my books until I found a photograph of one that looked almost the same as the one carved in stone right in front of me. It turned out that skulls and crossbones were meant as reminders that everyone dies and had nothing to do with pirates.

As I picked my way among the stones, the not-pirate symbols were everywhere. Then I discovered carvings of tipped-over hourglasses. That meant time had stopped for the person buried below. Several stones away, I spotted a winged hourglass. That meant time on earth was fleeting.

Then I came upon a carved butterfly. I had done a science report on butterflies a few months ago and learned all about cocoons and metamorphosis. So I thought a butterfly would symbolize rebirth. I was wrong again. According to one of Creelman's books, it meant a life cut short.

"Come and look at this one," I called to Merrilee, who had drifted into my zone.

She sidled over and inspected the carving by running her fingers over its wings. Then she said in a deadpan voice, "I think I've come across a secret code."

"Where?" I asked, peering closely at the butterfly.

"Not in the cemetery," she said, shaking her head. "In the mystery novel I signed out from the library last week. *The Purloined Parrot.* The one Loyola told us was anonymously donated."

"Well, sure," I said, stepping back from the gravestone. "Mystery books often have secret codes. And smoking guns and suspicious butlers and red herrings."

Where was she going with this?

"No, you don't get it," Merrilee said, rooting around in her knapsack. She pulled out the library's copy of *The Purloined Parrot*. She handed it to me. "Look on the dedication page."

I flipped to the page at the beginning of the book.

"'To my darling Arlene,'" I read out loud.

And then I noticed a list of words handwritten in pencil in the margin. The writing was cramped but tidy, and whenever the letter *a* occurred, it was written with a hood, as if it was typed, rather than how we were taught to print it, like a ball and stick. The words in the list were out of the ordinary but unconnected as far as I could tell: helicopter, flashlight, tripod, radiator, basket, orchid.

"Just looks like an unusual list of words, right?" Merrilee said.

I nodded.

"At first, I thought so, too. But then I noticed that each of these words first appeared in the same order in the novel. And then I remembered a book I had signed out a few months ago about writing secret codes. I did a project on it. One of the simplest types of codes is the classic book code.

"The classic book code," I repeated, trying to follow along.

"What you do is write down a secret message, then grab a book and find the first appearance of each of the words in the message in that book. Then you write down the word that is right before each of the words in your message. String those new words together in the same order to make the code. That's what this list of unusual words is. A code."

"Wait," I said. "You're saying that you found each of the words on this list inside the book, and then you wrote down the words that followed each of the words you found? Is that it?"

"Yes," she said. "And you know what? Those new words put together gave me *The Case of the Waylaid Water Gun*."

"The case of the waylaid water gun? Sounds like the title of another mystery book," I said.

"You're right," Merrilee said. "Turns out it is."

Except I wasn't following. The name of another mystery novel? So what! It was probably just some weird coincidence, like how all the grave markers that surrounded us were facing the same way.

Merrilee stopped nodding and scowled at my lack of enthusiasm.

"You still don't get it," she said with annoyance. She dug around in her knapsack and pulled out another book, which she handed to me.

"*The Case of the Waylaid Water Gun*," I said, reading the cover.

"Look at the dedication page," she said impatiently.

This time, I didn't read the dedication out loud. Instead, I immediately spotted another list in pencil. It was written in the same penmanship with the same letter *a*.

"So, you're going to have to read this book, too, just to get to the next message?" I asked, handing the novel back.

"Exactly!"

"Where's this going?" I asked. "All it sounds like is just a bunch of reading from one book to the next, like some kind of secret mystery book club."

"It's more than just books. I can feel it. I *genuinely* can," Merrilee said, pushing her glasses higher on her nose with a jab.

This from a girl who liked to spend outdoor time in cemeteries. Any minute now I expected her to admit that she had special powers and saw dead people or something equally disturbing.

I stood waiting.

"Still. Who's behind the codes?" I asked after a minute had passed without her admitting to anything.

Merrilee shrugged.

"Loyola said the book was donated anonymously, remember?" she said.

She tucked the book under her arm and returned her attention to the butterfly on the headstone I had spotted.

There was another long and awkward silence.

"Butterflies give me the creeps," she said at last.

I guessed we were done talking about secret codes. At least for now.

"Butterflies give you the creeps?" I repeated. "I thought girls loved butterflies, right after unicorns, ballerinas and mermaids."

"Not me," she said. "I find them creepy."

There we were, standing in an old cemetery, surrounded by ghosts galore, talking about secret codes written in anonymously donated mystery books, but it was *butterflies* that gave Merrilee the creeps. Good grief!

"What's so creepy about them?" I asked.

"They don't know who they are," she said. "One day they're a caterpillar with a million legs. The next day they're fluttering their wings."

"That's what makes them special," I argued.

"No, that's what makes them creepy," Merrilee insisted.

She took off her glasses, breathed on each lens, then rubbed them clean with a tissue from her pocket.

"Well, creepy or not, according to Creelman's book, a butterfly is a symbol for a short life."

"I rest my case," Merrilee said, putting her glasses back on. "Butterflies are creepy and sad."

I could tell that I wasn't going to win this pointless argument any time soon. Instead, I surveyed the cemetery, looking for Pascal. I spotted him in the far distance, a flash of brilliant light catching my eye. Obviously, he was still playing with his mirror.

"What section are you going to study next?" I asked Merrilee.

"Don't worry about me," she said, turning away.

She took off her jacket, laid it on the soggy ground, then plopped down and rested her back against the headstone with the carved butterfly. She opened *The Case of the Waylaid Water Gun* to where she had inserted a well-worn playing card — the Queen of Spades wearing a hand-drawn pair of glasses — and began to read.

"How are you going to get out of the quiz this time?" I asked point blank.

I did nothing to hide my bitterness.

"You'll see," she said dismissively, licking her index finger to flip a page. She didn't bother to look up.

"I'm going to head back," I reported, but Merrilee was already lost in her book, dead set on solving the next secret code.

I decided to make my way closer to the iron gate where Pascal was still flashing his mirror. I took an inventory of the symbols along the way to test myself. Weeping willow. Skull and crossbones. Crown. Dove. Urn. Skull and crossbones. Trumpet. Angel. Skull and crossbones. Grapevine. Candle. Wreath. Shell.

Then I came across a carved stone lamb. I froze. I had seen a lamb before, I was sure of it. But I couldn't think of where. Suddenly, the ground wobbled, and I had to grab a nearby grave marker to steady myself. I tried to call out, but I had no voice. The colors drained around me, and everything turned to black and white. Even the birds stopped singing. What was happening?

I felt a tap on my shoulder.

I screamed.

"Whoa," Pascal said. "Jumpy or what?"

Instead of feeling relief, I filled with rage. "Don't ever sneak up on me like that again!"

Even as I shouted, I knew I was overreacting. I turned away and bent over to take some deep breaths. Merrilee popped up from her hiding spot in the distance to see what was the matter.

"Sorry," Pascal said. "I didn't mean to scare you."

"I'm not scared," I barked back, probably sounding terrified. "I just don't like being sneaked up on, that's all."

I glanced at Pascal. He stood holding his stack of books, his knapsack at his feet. I was dead certain he could hear my heart pounding from where he stood, and I thought he was going to make fun of me. I braced for it.

"Want to quiz each other on symbols before the Brigade gets back?"

I paused. There wasn't a trace of meanness in his voice. He really did want to work on our assignment. Maybe he couldn't hear my pounding heart after all.

"Sure," I said, grateful that the colors in the cemetery had returned and that Merrilee had sat back down.

We found a nearby bench and laid the books on

symbolism between us. Pascal started by opening up one of his and pointing to a picture of a headstone, while I told him what I thought the symbol meant. We went back and forth like that until Pascal grew bored and completely changed the subject.

"They've picked the locker for the time capsule," he announced, as he stretched his arms.

"Really?" I said.

The time-capsule program has been going on at Queensview Elementary for even longer than community service duty. Every seven years, someone in grade six gets picked to turn his or her locker into a time capsule at the end of the school year.

"Whose locker?" I asked.

"Marcus Papadopoulos's."

Marcus was in my science class, and he recently got top marks for the ant farm project he had made out of old plastic jewel cases, aluminum foil and duct tape. Not a single ant escaped, much to our disappointment.

"Wonder what he'll leave in his locker," I mused.

"If it were me," Pascal said, "I'd leave my collection of Phentex slippers."

"What kind of slippers?"

"Phentex. It's a type of yarn that never ever wears out, believe me. Stronger than tombstone marble, that's for sure. My grandmother knits me a pair for my birthday every year. I must have a hundred pairs by now." Pascal closed his book. "What would you leave?"

I took a minute to answer. It was a tough question. We had been told that time capsules usually contain items such as school supplies, photographs, journals and books. Sometimes clothing is left in them. Or seeds. Or small gadgets. I would want to put in things that said a lot about me, but that I wouldn't miss. The thing about the school's time-capsule program is that you don't get the items back. The locker gets locked and a plaque is placed on it. Then it stays sealed, only to be reopened fifty years later.

"I might put in a collection of t-shirts with my favorite sayings," I said, pointing to the one I was wearing about footprints on the moon.

Pascal was eyeing my t-shirt when something else caught his attention behind me.

"Here they come," he warned under his breath.

I looked. The Brigade had marched their way past the iron gate and were headed straight to our section. We stood.

"Merrilee!" Pascal called.

Merrilee got up, saw what was happening and gathered her belongings.

"Quiz time," Creelman announced. "Put the books away."

"Actually," Merrilee replied, having just joined the group, "Loyola asked me to remind you that we'll need to return the books early today. A genealogy tour group is dropping by the library this afternoon to have a look at them. That's why I stacked mine ready to go near the gate."

I gave Merrilee a suspicious look. She had failed to mention any of this to me when we talked about her mystery novel with the handwritten secret code or her inexplicable dislike of butterflies.

"That's right, the tour," Creelman said, his eyebrows crowding together. "I forgot it was scheduled for today."

"I could return everyone's books right now if you like," Merrilee offered helpfully.

Did she just give me a wink?

"Good idea," Creelman said. "In the meantime, we'll quiz the rest of the group."

The rest of the group? I looked at Pascal, and Pascal looked at me.

Merrilee collected our books and practically skipped away, whistling a cheerful tune.

"Follow me," Creelman ordered, and we did.

Reluctantly.

He worked his way from gravestone to gravestone, pointing to various carvings with his cane.

"What does this mean?" he demanded periodically.

"Liberty."

"Cycle of life."

"Eternal sleep."

"Passage of time."

"End of the family line."

"Triumph over death."

"Fallen soldier."

"Dawn of life."

"Victory."

"Hope."

Hope was my favorite — a winged angel kneeling beside a ship's anchor.

And I had to admit that between the two of us, Pascal and I had become pretty good with symbols.

But Creelman was not the type to hand out gold stars. He barely nodded with each right answer before immediately striding to the next gravestone, determined to trip us up. Finally, Wooster warned Creelman about the time by pointing to his pocket watch. It was getting late.

"Fine," Creelman said, glaring at us as if it was our fault.

We made our way back to the iron gate.

"See you boys next week," Creelman said grudgingly.

The Brigade marched one way down the street. Pascal vamoosed in the opposite direction.

I lingered at the gate for a few minutes, expecting to see Merrilee pop out of the library any minute, now that the coast was clear.

Instead, a busload of seniors pulled up to the curb, blocking my view. I watched as they climbed off the bus, while Loyola charged down the library steps to greet them. I could hear her laughter even from where I stood.

I turned back to look at the rows of markers. From this distance, all the symbols we had carefully memorized had disappeared. The gravestones now looked the same, an endless gray sea, patiently marking time. It was only up close that the stones could whisper their stories to anyone who'd listen.

And then I remembered the grave marker that had given me such a shock — the one with the carved lamb. I scanned the cemetery to see if I could spot its location, but that marker remained hidden among the silent stony crowd.

What was it about the lamb? What did it mean? Where had I seen it before? My stomach lurched. There could only be one place — the cemetery at Ferndale.

Ferndale was the nearby town where we had lived when I was little. It was where the accident with the orange rubber ball had happened, the accident that had been giving me nightmares ever since then, the accident that had ended just like all the stories ended at Twillingate Cemetery.

My mouth went dry.

Three

Mapping Plots

HERE'S HOW I get by. I bury thoughts I don't want to deal with deep inside and store them in a place that I pretend looks like my dad's garage workshop. It's a real mess in there — half-finished projects abandoned and piled in the corners, workbenches covered in assorted hand tools that rarely make it back to the toolbox, overflowing garbage cans, and bent nails scattered across the floor. But my dad believes that the mess magically disappears whenever he shuts the garage door.

That's what I have — a garage door. I just have to remember to keep it shut.

Only every once in a while, I accidentally leave the door open. When that happens, nothing is hidden.

Last night, I had the nightmare again. It started and ended the exact same way, no matter how much I wanted to change it.

I am sitting on the front steps eating a popsicle, checking out a scab on my knee. The cement is warm beneath me. I can smell fresh grass. The lawn has just been cut, and my dad rolls his mower to the backyard. A screen door squeaks, and it is Dennis from the brick house beside us. I wave. He has an orange rubber ball.

No!

I'm not going to do this now.

I pull on the garage door with all my might and it slams shut.

This time.

It was Wednesday afternoon again. Another blue-sky day. Merrilee stood waiting by the iron gate in her red plastic bunnies-and-carrots jacket, and as soon as she spotted me, she rifled through her knapsack to show me something.

"Here," she said, handing me a book.

"Hello, Merrilee," I replied. "I'm fine, thanks for asking."

"No time for that," she said. "Check this out before the Brigade gets here."

I read the title of her book. *To Catch a Bicycle Thief.*

"Let me guess. There's a secret code handwritten on the dedication page."

"Hurry up and look," Merrilee said.

Sure enough, there was a penciled list of seven words in the margin. Same funny letter *a*'s: tortoise, gargoyle, birdbath, cherub, chimes, fountain, dory.

"The last mystery book was fantastic. I could hardly put it down. It led me to this title, which looks just as good."

I read the blurb on the back cover out loud.

"'A book with so many plot twists, you'll be tied up in knots.'"

I liked plot twists.

I opened to chapter 1 and read the first line to her.

"'The sun made shadows on the face of the moon that were so deep, they could trip an astronaut.'"

Trip-able shadows. I liked that, too.

"Not bad," I admitted. "Maybe I'll read it when you're done."

She rifled through her knapsack again and pulled out two more library copies of the same book, just as Pascal joined us.

"What do you have there?" he asked.

"Books with the latest code," said Merrilee.

"Right. The secret code," Pascal said. "You still don't know who's behind this?"

"No. But I'm getting closer. Do you want a copy?"

"*To Catch a Bicycle Thief*," Pascal read. Then he flipped to the dedication page that contained the secret code. "Seven words," he said. "Shouldn't be that hard."

"And there are plot twists," I added.

"Okay, why not. I'm in," Pascal said.

"Me, too," I said.

I put my copy into my knapsack. If I woke up from the nightmare again tonight, at least I would have something interesting to read.

"Here they come," I said, having glanced up to see the Brigade parading across the street from the library, with Creelman in the lead.

As he marched along, Creelman jabbed his cane at a mail truck that had pulled up too close to the crosswalk for his liking.

"Maybe we're actually going to fix some gravestones today like the sign-up sheet promised," Pascal said.

"Not likely," I said when I saw who was pulling up the rear. "Wooster's holding clipboards."

"How many more weeks of this?" Pascal lamented.

"Ten," Merrilee chirped. "But at least now you've got something to read as soon as they leave."

"Oh, sure! Reading's okay for you," I said. "But have you noticed that Pascal and I keep getting hit with quizzes?"

"No," Merrilee said dryly. "I've been too busy reading."

Then we all clammed up because the Brigade had arrived.

"Good afternoon," Creelman said, but I was sure he didn't mean it. "Ready for Lesson 3?"

"Are we going to fix gravestones today?" Pascal asked against all odds.

Why? *Why* did he do that? Pascal knew there was no chance of repairing today. He could see the clipboards as well as I could. Good grief!

Creelman didn't answer. Instead, he marched over to a nearby stone and pointed to it with his cane.

"Today's three simple rules," he announced. "One, you must never repair a grave marker if you don't know what type of stone it is. Two, you must never repair a grave marker unless you can identify the parts of the stone that you need to repair. Three, you must never repair a grave marker unless you can map out where it is in the cemetery to make a record of what you've done."

Types, parts, maps. I imagined another deadly long afternoon ahead of me.

"This," Creelman said, tapping a nearby stone, "is sandstone. As you can see, it's reddish brown. Great for carving, but crumbles over time." He moved to another stone that was much thinner. "This is slate. It's blue gray, but it's brittle and can peel in layers. These two types of stones are found in the oldest parts of our cemetery. They came from nearby quarries."

"Over there," he said, waving his cane in the direction of a cluster of whiter stones. "Marble. You already know that marble is soft, so it's great for sculpture, but erosion takes its toll. Over time, the surface becomes grainy, like sugar. Do you know what that's called?"

We shook our heads. Even Pascal.

"Sugaring. You'll also find white bronze, which is

really a metal called zinc. Those markers never seem to age. Even lichen stays away. And way over there in the north end, past the first hedgerow, are the granites. Granite is speckled and very hard to carve by hand. Nowadays, lasers are used to etch images into the stone. You'll find granite in the newer parts of the cemetery."

I could see the polished pink and black stones in the distance. They were lined up more precisely than the markers in the section we were standing in.

"Where are the white crosses?" Pascal asked.

Creelman stared at him.

"You know, the ones made out of wood, like you see in cowboy movies," Pascal explained. He held up his two pointer fingers and crossed them, as if he were fending off a vampire.

Merrilee did not look amused, possibly because vampires ran in her family.

"This isn't a pioneer cemetery," Creelman growled, "but if you're really interested, go to Ferndale. Their cemetery has a pioneer section close to three hundred years old."

Ferndale. I clutched my knapsack. I could not hear their next words because I was struggling to keep my garage door shut.

"Derek! Are you coming?"

I snapped to. The Brigade had moved off to another section, Merrilee in tow. Pascal stood halfway between them and me.

"You okay?" he asked in a voice that told me I looked like death warmed over.

"Sure," I lied.

But my hair was sticking to my forehead. I fished out my water bottle from my knapsack and took a big swig before we rejoined the Brigade.

"Did you hear that last bit?" Creelman demanded as soon as we caught up.

"No," I muttered, feeling foolish and sweating all over again.

"I said that there are three basic shapes of gravestones. Upright, flat and obelisk."

Even as I struggled to pay attention, I glanced around to see if the carved lamb was anywhere near me.

It wasn't.

"Let's start with the uprights. The main part is called the tablet. The tablets from our oldest stones usually have some kind of curved top that's meant to look like a door to the other side."

Pascal took a step toward one.

Don't do it, Pascal, I thought as loudly as I could. Don't do it!

But to no surprise, he couldn't read my mind. He walked around to the back of a nearby upright grave marker, looking for who knows what behind that door. Creelman ignored him. He was getting good at it.

"The top curved part is called the lunette. These stones also have side pillars, or borders, to frame the door, like you see in churches and temples. At the top of the pillars you'll see circular finials. The last part is the face of the gravestone. That's where you'll find the inscription, the place where the name and dates are recorded."

"Inscription," Pascal repeated. "I thought that was when the government forced people to become soldiers."

"I think you mean *conscription*," Merrilee corrected.

"Isn't that what a doctor fills out on a pad of paper so that you can get medicine at the drugstore?"

"That's a *prescription*," she said, pushing her glasses up and looking away.

One thing about Pascal. He could be counted on to keep my mind off things.

"Moving on," Creelman said, paying no heed to Pascal with remarkable persistence. "The flat stones that look like tables usually cover an underground family vault, or tomb. Some have chests sitting on the table-tops, but it is a mistake to think that people are placed inside those chests. The chests only mark the site of the tomb below, where everyone's buried in the ground."

Pascal walked over to a nearby tabletop for closer inspection.

"Some people think that the horizontal stones were used before we had public cemeteries. You would bury a family member in a field, then place a large stone on top to keep the animals away," Creelman explained. "They were called wolf stones."

I looked around again. There were fewer of those than of the door-shaped grave markers, and they all had more than one name on them, just like Creelman said.

"Pop quiz," Creelman announced. "Who is entombed inside this chest?"

He just told us that no one was, that everyone was buried below in the family vault, but I knew Pascal would steer us in the wrong direction.

Sure enough, Pascal was about to read the names out loud when I cut in.

"No one," I answered boldly. "They're buried below."

Creelman nodded grudgingly, perhaps annoyed that I had rescued Pascal from his latest trap.

"Lastly, the obelisks." Creelman pointed to the tall pointy columns in the distance. "These were popular in the nineteenth century, when people became fascinated with ancient pharaohs discovered in tombs in Egypt."

It looked to me as if the obelisks were for those who liked to show off their wealth like the pharaohs did.

"Okay, the last part of today's lesson is how to read a map," Creelman said.

On cue, Wooster advanced with his clipboards and handed one to each of us. The clipboards had a map and a second sheet of paper with a list of numbers and blanks to fill out.

"When you record information about the gravestone you are working on, you need to be sure you know where it is located on the map. There can be no mistakes," Creelman warned, wagging his finger at us.

I studied my map. It marked the boundaries of the cemetery and where the iron gate was located. It showed all the stone walls and paths and major groves of trees. Some sections of the map were marked with area names: Garden of Angels, Garden of Memories, Children's Garden, Serenity Lookout, Veterans' Hill and Potter's Meadow. There was a compass drawn in the corner, pointing which way was north. And the map was filled with clusters of tiny boxes, each box numbered. Every once in a while, there was a box with a pointy top marking an obelisk.

"Turn to the second page," Creelman ordered. It was the sheet filled with numbers and blanks beside them. "You will spend the rest of the afternoon locating the grave marker for each number. When you find the grave marker, write down the name of the person buried, the year they died, the type of stone and the style of grave marker. Got it?"

Pascal rotated his map around and around, bending his head this way and that. "Which way do I point this map?" he finally asked.

"Here are two facts you can count on," Creelman said. "Moss always grows on the north side of trees, and gravestones always face west."

"Always?" Pascal repeated in awe.

Creelman heaved a sigh.

"No. But they mostly face west, and bodies are laid behind the stones, with their heads to the west and their feet to the east. Ministers and priests like to be buried the opposite way, to face their flock."

"Flock? As in birds?" Pascal asked, turning to me.

I decided to pull a Creelman and ignore Pascal by asking my own question.

"I understand why ministers and priests would want to face members of their church, but why do church members want to face east?" I asked.

"What rises in the east?" Creelman asked, waving his hand toward the eastern part of the cemetery.

From where I stood, I thought the obvious answer was "ghosts," but I knew enough not to say that out loud.

"Here's a hint. It's the only star in our galaxy," Creelman added.

"Oh," I said with relief, "the sun!"

"Correct," Creelman said. "The dawn of a new day." Then he hesitated. "Are you interested in astronomy?"

"The moon and the stars? Sure," I said.

I wished I had been wearing last week's t-shirt, the one about footprints on the moon. Instead, I glanced down and was horrified to see what I had selected. *I'd turn back if I were you.*

"Have you ever been to a planetarium?" he asked.

"No," I admitted, somehow feeling as if this was my fault.

Creelman's face fell as quickly as it had risen. He

turned his attention to his cronies, and they nodded toward the iron gate.

I looked at my list. There must have been twenty-five numbers. This was going to take an eternity. Then I wondered how Merrilee was going to get out of it.

The Brigade marched out the gate without a backward glance.

"Well, boys," Merrilee said brightly. "I believe I have a secret code to solve."

With that she parked herself beside a nearby obelisk and opened *To Catch a Bicycle Thief* to a page where she pulled out her Queen of Spades bookmark.

Merrilee annoyed me, but I couldn't tell if it was because as sure as the sun rises in the east, she would somehow manage to get out of today's quiz, or that she was already chapters ahead in her book and seemed dead set on solving the mystery novel code before me or Pascal.

I looked at my list again. Maybe if I could cut my work in half, I could catch up to Merrilee in the reading. After all, I was a pretty fast reader myself. And lately, I had plenty of time to kill in the dead of night.

"Hey, Pascal. How about I do the first half of the list, and you do the second half. Then we'll share answers."

"Deal," Pascal said with relief, and off he went.

I gave Merrilee a smug look, but she was already lost in her book.

I spent the rest of the afternoon traipsing back and

forth between the rows of gravestones and filling in the blanks. It was tedious and never-ending.

But thankfully, I did not come across the gravestone with the lamb.

The Brigade returned just before quitting time.

"Let's see your answers," Creelman demanded.

Pascal and I handed over our clipboards to Wooster and Preeble. I kept an eye on Merrilee to see what she would do, having spent the entire afternoon reading and dead to the world.

Merrilee boldly handed over her clipboard to Creelman.

Then, amazingly, all three members of the Brigade began to mark our answers, Merrilee's included!

How had she done it? I was certain that she hadn't moved from that obelisk all afternoon!

Merrilee gave me a small smile as the Brigade handed back our tests.

Pascal and I each got four wrong, three of them from Pascal's section I might add.

Merrilee got a perfect score.

"Not bad," Creelman said gruffly to her.

As soon as the Brigade left through the iron gate for the day and was out of earshot, I pounced on Merrilee.

"How'd you do it?" I demanded.

"Simple," she said. "When I was in the library signing out copies of *To Catch a Bicycle Thief*, I found the answer sheet in the photocopy room. Creelman must have made copies for Wooster and Preeble, and he left the master list behind."

"So all you had to do was copy out the answers," Pascal said. "Awesome."

"It's not awesome!" I snapped. "We're killing ourselves out here, and she keeps getting away with murder."

"Come on," Pascal said, looking at his quiz. "It beats getting four wrong. If I had seen that master list, I would have done the same thing."

"Really?" I said with sarcasm. "Is that your motto?"

"What do you mean?" Pascal asked.

"If I made you a t-shirt, would it read, *I'd have done the same thing*?"

Pascal grinned. "I'd love that!"

"And if you made a t-shirt for me, what would it say?" Merrilee asked.

I ignored her question. I was still mad at how she had gotten away with cheating.

"You know," I warned. "You're not going to have a clue when it comes time to fixing gravestones."

"Maybe not. But I've already solved the first clue in *To Catch a Bicycle Thief*."

She dug out her copy and flipped it open.

"Check it out," she said.

Pascal and I leaned in and read the word she was pointing to.

"The first word in this book's secret code is 'tortoise.'"

She slid her finger to the word that followed "tortoise."

Pascal read that word out loud. "'Trevor.'"

"Not many books would start with the name Trevor," I said. "Why not do a quick library search on titles with Trevor in them. Then you could cheat the code, too."

"Already tried it," Merrilee said, ignoring my attempt at insulting her.

I looked at Merrilee with astonishment.

She shrugged. "When I ducked out to return the master list to the library, I did a quick search."

I couldn't believe that I had not seen her leave the cemetery, especially in that red plastic bunnies-and-carrots jacket of hers! Had I just been too busy with the exercise to notice?

No. A more likely explanation was that I was too tired to see things clearly. I hadn't gotten a good night's sleep in ages on account of my nightmares.

"So, this code is not going to lead to another mystery book like the last ones?" Pascal asked.

"No," Merrilee said. "This one's different."

Four

Cleaning Stones

I am sitting on the front steps eating a popsicle. There's a scab on my knee. The cement is warm beneath me, and the grass smells sweet. My dad is rolling his mower to the backyard. A screen door squeaks, and it is my neighbor, Dennis. I wave. He has an orange rubber ball.

I scarf down the rest of my popsicle and put the stick in my pocket. I am saving sticks to make a cowboy corral. I already have the plastic horses.

Dennis cuts across the newly mown grass. He kicks the ball to me. I try to kick it back, but I miss. He laughs. I laugh, too, as I scramble to get the ball. I kick it to him. He misses. We laugh. We go back and forth, back and forth. The sun is warm. The grass is sweet. The orange ball is tricky.

Back and forth, back and forth. We miss most

of the kicks, and we are laughing. I can hear the lawnmower in the backyard. It is loud.

We are the only ones playing outside on our little street, with the young trees just planted and the houses brand-new. It is too hot for most people, and there is no shade. They stay indoors where it is cool and they can make ice cubes. We are the only ones outside, except for my dad, who is cutting the lawn in the backyard, and the car that is driving down our street.

I can hear my dad's lawnmower, but I do not hear the car. Dennis does not hear the car, either.

I kick the ball. Hard. Dennis misses. He chases after the orange ball. It bounces across the lawn and onto the street.

No! I slammed the garage door shut, but not before I sat bolt upright in my bed with my heart pounding and my sheets soaked in sweat.

I could hear my ragged breathing through my tight throat and chest. Deep breaths, I told myself. In, out. In, out.

I turned on my bed lamp. My alarm clock said it was 2:07 in the morning. I was wide awake. *To Catch a Bicycle Thief* was on my night table. I opened it to where I last left off. I was looking for the next word in the code. By 2:46 I had found it in chapter 9.

First word: Trevor.

Second word: Tower.

Trevor Tower.

Who was Trevor Tower?

I flipped to the end of my book. Only three more chapters to go. I turned my back to my alarm clock and forged ahead. I don't remember what time I finally got to sleep that night, but in the morning when I woke up, the first thing I did was put the sheet of paper where I had written the solved code into my knapsack.

For once, I couldn't wait for cemetery duty that afternoon so that I could share my results with Pascal and Merrilee.

"Hey," I said as soon I got to the iron gate.

Pascal and Merrilee had already arrived.

"I solved the code," I boasted.

"We did, too," Merrilee said. "Trevor Tower keeps secrets, twenty-eight, thirty-four, eighteen."

"Oh," I said, a bit deflated.

"So what do you think it means?" Pascal asked. "We already know it's not the title of another mystery book."

"The other codes. Did they have numbers?" I asked Merrilee.

"No," she said. "They didn't."

"And you don't know who Trevor Tower is?" I asked.

"No idea," Merrilee said. "But he's not an author. I checked that out at the library, too. So this is definitely the last code to solve."

"Trevor Tower keeps secrets," I repeated. "Twenty-eight, thirty-four, eighteen."

"Here comes the Brigade," Merrilee reported.

We all turned to watch the trio navigate the crosswalk and plow through the gate. They carried clipboards and, for the first time, buckets.

"What do you think we'll be doing today?" Pascal asked dryly. "Surely not cleaning gravestones, even though that's what I thought we had signed up to do."

"Good afternoon," Creelman said when the Brigade had assembled in front of us. "Today's lesson: cleaning gravestones."

"Really? That's great!" Pascal exclaimed. "But before we begin, do you know Trevor Tower?"

Creelman frowned. He set down his bucket and flipped through sheets of paper on his clipboard. Preeble and Wooster did the same.

"No," Creelman said. "He's not listed as buried here. Why are you asking about Trevor Tower?" Creelman inquired reluctantly.

Merrilee shot Pascal a warning look.

"No reason," Pascal said, but the way he kept bouncing from foot to foot told the entire Brigade otherwise.

Creelman scowled while he worked out whether to pursue his line of questions, move on to the lesson of the day or go for a cigarette.

"As I was saying," Creelman finally continued, "today we're cleaning gravestones."

Pascal and Merrilee fell into a silent line beside me.

"The first thing you must figure out is what type of

material you need to clean off the gravestone."

Creelman held up his hand and began to count down on his fingers.

"There are five common materials that plague markers. Soot. Dirt. Organics such as lichens and moss. Stains caused by metal or oil. And salt."

Creelman picked up his bucket.

"Most of our cleaning will be to remove organics."

This time, I dared to ask a question.

"Why are lichens and moss a problem for stone?"

"Moss stains, and its root system pries stone apart. Lichens hold water on the stone, delaying evaporation. This makes the stone prey to frost damage."

I nodded. I had no idea moss and lichen could be so evil.

"In this cemetery, we use the least aggressive cleaning method along with good clear water. And we always clean from the bottom up. This avoids stains from streaking down on the area you've just cleaned. Now, grab your buckets."

The Brigade handed the buckets to us.

"Each bucket has a set of rubber gloves, a sponge and a soft bristle brush. Put the gloves on and go fill your buckets from that spigot," Creelman said, pointing his cane to a nearby tap that the groundskeepers used for water. "Then select a gravestone from these three rows. We'll come by with a cleaner, depending on the type of material you'll need to remove."

We went to fill our buckets, then wandered among the rows to pick a gravestone. I chose a slate one that belonged to a man who died over two hundred years ago. He had a double grave marker for him and his wife, with two sets of angel heads and wings carved at the top. His name and dates were filled in on one side, but curiously, the other half remained blank.

When Creelman came by with my cleaner, I asked, "What do you think happened here?"

I pointed to the blank side of the stone.

"I guess his wife was dead set against being buried next to him," Creelman said.

I started to laugh until I saw that Creelman continued to scowl, as if he hadn't said anything funny at all.

I sobered up pretty quickly.

"What's the cleaner you've added to my water?" I asked, getting back to business.

"You've got some organic growth there, so you'll be using a cleaner we like that is biodegradable, has no salt, no bleaches and only a touch of ammonia."

I put on my gloves and picked up my sponge.

"Go easy on the stone. Remember to start at the bottom."

"Right," I said.

I got to work. And believe me, I started at the bottom.

As I cleaned the stone, I wondered about the man buried below. The grave marker told me very little. His name was Enoch Pettypiece. He lived to be 33 years, 5 months and 8 days old. His stone also read, *He was an affectionate husband, tender parent, lived respected and died lamented.*

If Enoch Pettypiece *had* been an affectionate husband, then Creelman had gotten it wrong. Maybe Enoch Pettypiece was killed, and his distraught wife was carried off by canoe to Quebec, to be later rescued by missionaries, but died of a strange ailment before she ever got a chance to return home. Very sad.

I reread the gravestone and noticed that the word *affectionate* had a carved box around it, as if the word had been changed or reworked by relatives after Enoch Pettypiece died. Maybe Creelman was on to something after all.

I tried to think what the original word might have read as I looked at the blank side of the double marker where the details about his wife should have been.

He was a *dastardly* husband?

He was a *penny-pinching* husband?

He was a *forgettable* husband?

If any of that was the case, then his wife would be having the last say for all eternity. Enoch's family could change the word all they wanted, but she was not going to be buried next to *him*.

Then again, maybe it was just a typo. Maybe Enoch Pettypiece was a school teacher who was forever correcting spelling mistakes on his students' homework.

When he realized that there was a typo on his own gravestone, he haunted the stone carver until the carver returned to the burial site and corrected the spelling of *affectionate* so that Enoch could finally rest in peace.

I sat back on my heels, enjoying the different scenarios, any one of which could be true. I decided that if I were to make Enoch Pettypiece a t-shirt, it would read, *Dead men tell no stories.*

It was some time later, when I stood to stretch, that I noticed the Brigade had left for their coffee break. I walked over to where Pascal was working.

"How's it going?" I asked.

"Okay," Pascal said. "At least we're finally doing some real work."

Pascal paused from scrubbing.

"I was thinking about the code. Trevor Tower keeps secrets. Twenty-eight, thirty-four, eighteen. What could it mean?"

I shrugged. "The name sounds like someone around our age. Trevor is pretty modern. Not like Enoch."

"Enoch?"

"That's my guy's name on the gravestone I'm working on."

Pascal sat back on his heels.

"You're probably right. Trevor Tower keeps secrets. Twenty-eight, thirty-four, eighteen. Someone our age."

"I said someone *around* our age. Trevor Tower could be in high school or even older, like Loyola Louden, for all we know. He might not even be a student. I just meant that he has a name you'd hear today. Not like Enoch."

"What about the numbers?" Pascal asked. "Twenty-eight. Thirty-four. Eighteen."

"I guess we should ask ourselves what has three numbers," I said.

"Telephone area codes," Pascal suggested. "They have three numbers."

"Except that area codes use numbers from zero to nine. These numbers are too big."

"How about fertilizer? Fertilizer bags always have three numbers."

"Fertilizer? Really, Pascal?"

"Sure. The numbers tell you how much nitrogen, phosphorus and potassium are in it. Those three things are needed to make plants grow."

"How do you know that?"

"My mom showed me at the plant store."

"I still think fertilizer is a stretch," I said. Then I remembered buying some sunglasses with my dad. "Sunglasses always come with three numbers."

"They do?" Pascal asked.

"On the inside of the arm of the left temple. The three numbers measure the length of the eye piece, the length of the bridge between the two eye pieces, and the length of the arm."

"Well, I think sunglasses are just as much of a stretch

as fertilizer," Pascal said. "What could sunglasses have to do with someone named Trevor Tower who keeps secrets?"

He had a point.

"Fair enough," I said.

We sat in silence for a while, pondering the possibilities.

Twenty-eight. Thirty-four. Eighteen.

"Doesn't that sound like a combination lock to you?" Pascal said.

"Yes, actually, it does," I admitted.

Good grief! Could Pascal be on to something?

"So whoever Trevor Tower is, maybe he has a locker," Pascal continued. "And where do we find lockers?"

"Schools, mostly," I said.

"Bingo," Pascal said. "Trevor Tower *must* be a student."

"Only he's quite a few years older than us because we haven't heard of him," I said, confirming my earlier speculation.

"But if he's from around here, he might have gone to our school when he was younger. I think we should check it out," Pascal said.

"Check what out?" Merrilee asked.

Somehow, she had sneaked up on us without a sound, vampire-like.

"What do you have there?" I asked, pointing to the bucket she was carrying in an attempt to distract her.

"Some kind of special detergent that's good for dirt," she replied. "Check what out?"

I didn't want to tell Merrilee about our theory. She would probably poke all kinds of holes in it just for sport.

"Check out the gravestone I'm cleaning. It's blank."

I shot Pascal a look that said, "Keep quiet."

He did, but not without a confused tilt of his head.

"Blank?" Merrilee repeated, setting her bucket down.

"Come and see," I said.

I led her and Pascal over to where I had been working on the double gravestone.

We stood in front of the blank side.

"Looks like Enoch didn't die happily ever after," Merrilee said.

"Where is your wife, good sir?" Pascal asked Enoch.

No answer. Just birds singing in the trees.

"Twenty-eight. Thirty-four. Eighteen," Merrilee said. "Sounds like a combination lock to me."

"That's what we were thinking!" Pascal exclaimed, wheeling around to face her.

I shot him a glare, but he was already too busy comparing notes with Merrilee.

"So we need to find out who Trevor Tower is and where he keeps his locker."

"Agreed," Merrilee said.

"Just a second now," I interrupted. "Our plan is to

find out who Trevor Tower is and then break into his locker?"

The two stared at me.

"Doesn't that sound a little crazy to you? I mean, first of all, breaking into someone's locker must be illegal or something. And even if we do, what are we hoping to find?"

"Who knows," Pascal said with a shrug. "That's what we need to find out."

"There could be anything in a locker," I argued. "Stolen property. Rotting lunches. His wife's skeleton," I said, pointing to Enoch's grave marker. "Anything!"

"What's your point?" Pascal asked.

"*That's* my point!" I said. I looked to Merrilee for support, but she was studying Enoch's inscription.

"Merrilee," I said. "You're not serious about tracking down Trevor Tower or his locker, are you?"

"Do you think this was because of a typo?" she asked, running her fingertips over the carved box around *affectionate*.

"Forget about Enoch," I demanded. "We should think about what we're doing here."

"Cleaning grave markers?" she asked with a smirk.

"You know what I mean! Following a secret code that might lead us to someone's locker. It could be dangerous."

"True," she said, straightening up. "Let's just take it one step at a time. We'll figure out who Trevor Tower is first. And we won't open any locker until we're sure about what we're doing."

"Famous last words," I muttered.

"Well, you don't have to help. Pascal and I can continue on our own."

That got me. I wasn't keen on getting into trouble, but I didn't want to be left out, either.

"So you're saying that you're not worried. Not in the least?" I asked.

"Curious, yes. Worried, no."

She returned her attention to Enoch.

"Pascal," I said, turning to face him. "Think about it. Someone, and we don't even know who, has been writing secret codes in the margins of mystery books in the library. We've stumbled across the codes, solved the last one, and now we think we should figure out who Trevor Tower is. But maybe the codes weren't meant for us to discover. Maybe the codes were supposed to be for someone else, and all we're going to do is get in the way. Or worse!"

"Say! Do you think the Brigade has anything to do with the codes?" Pascal asked, clearly unfazed by my dire warning.

"Who, Creelman? Preeble? Wooster?" I asked. "Why would you think that?"

"I can't figure out why they're dead set on maintaining this graveyard," Pascal said. "Year after year, they accept students for cemetery duty, and the work is endless. Maybe this cemetery thing is a sham. Maybe the Brigade really spend their time watching students solve secret codes they've set up. In fact," Pascal said, dropping his voice to a whisper, "maybe they're watching us right now."

He and I scanned the gate and the surroundings while Merrilee rolled her eyes. Although there were plenty of people walking along the sidewalk past the cemetery, and a few going in and out of the library across the street, members of the Brigade were nowhere to be seen.

I thought back to the rainy day we first met Creelman, with his ancient yellowed notes and noisy table pounding. He didn't seem the type to be writing secret codes. And as for Preeble and Wooster, I had barely heard them utter a peep. It was next to impossible to imagine them communicating by any means, including secret codes.

Merrilee cut in.

"None of the Brigade have anything to do with the codes," she said matter-of-factly.

"How do you know?" I asked.

"I've compared samples of their writing with the codes. There's no match."

"Samples of their writing," I repeated. "Where did you get those from?"

"Their clipboards," she replied. "Their letter *a*'s look nothing like the letter *a* in the codes."

Pascal whistled softly.

"Impressive," he said.

But I didn't think it was impressive at all. Merrilee's quiet sleuthing abilities kept me on edge. And Pascal's bull-in-a-china-shop approach to everything kept me cringing.

I changed my mind. If I were to make a t-shirt for Pascal, it would read, *I do all my own stunts*. As for Merrilee, hers would read, *Ask me about my evil plot*.

"So, you're dead set on finding out who Trevor Tower is?" I asked, already knowing the answer.

"That's the plan," said the bull in the china shop.

The quiet sleuth didn't answer. She stared intently at the blank side of Enoch's grave marker. I took her stony silence to mean "yes."

"Fine," I said reluctantly, but only because I thought I could steer them to a safe place, at least for now. "Let's start by asking around our school."

Five

———

Sacred Grounds Cafe

I WAS WALKING ALONG Tulip Street, scouting out potential ideas for Mother's Day, when I spotted Creelman leaving the medical clinic where I had gone for my pink eye. I recognized the trench coat he was wearing from the first day we had met him in the library. His pockets were probably still stuffed with crinkled yellowed notes.

I stopped in my tracks and then stepped behind a florist's sidewalk display to watch where he would head.

Creelman did not look left or right. Instead, he made a beeline to a nearby trash can and pitched something into it. Then he marched down Tulip Street toward the library and cemetery.

I followed.

When I walked by the trash can, I peered inside. An opened package of cigarettes lay on top of the garbage, its health warning printed in ugly black letters.

So, Creelman was still trying to quit. I wondered if that was why he was grumpy all the time.

We both kept walking along Tulip Street, me trailing about a block and a half behind him and his cane. I don't know why I was so interested in his whereabouts. Boredom, maybe.

Creelman stopped only a few times along the way — once to tie his shoe, once to look into a storefront window that displayed used books, and once to stand aside to let three kids fly by on their skateboards.

Each time he stopped, I crouched, first behind a mailbox, then a lamppost and then a bicycle rack. And even from the spots where I hid, I could tell he was scowling, his cotton-ball eyebrows a dead giveaway.

At last, he came to the coffee shop near the cemetery. The sign of the shop read, *Sacred Grounds Cafe*. But he didn't duck inside like I expected.

Instead, he heaved the door open, spun around to face me and called out, "Are you coming, or what?"

I stayed put and attempted to turn invisible. Maybe he wasn't talking to me.

"Derek," he growled. "I haven't got all day."

He held the door open.

I slowly stood up from behind the bicycle rack. Good grief!

"Hello," I muttered when I was in earshot.

Creelman waved me into the cafe.

"Over there," he said, pointing to a booth in the corner next to the window. "I like the view outside."

I turned to look at the view. It was Twillingate Cemetery.

I slid into the booth while trying to decide if what I was feeling was embarrassment, terror, fascination or a mix of all three.

A waitress came by with the menus.

"And how's my favorite customer?" she asked, giving Creelman a wink.

"Hungry," he replied. "How's the meat loaf?"

"The same," she said. "Why don't you try something new? A nice bowl of lamb stew? A three-cheese omelet? Lasagna?"

"Meat loaf will do," Creelman said, handing back the menu without even looking at it.

"One meat loaf," the waitress repeated. She did not bother to write down his order.

"And you?" she said, turning to me with a hopeful smile. "What would you like?"

The only money I had with me was for a gift for Mother's Day.

"Just water for me," I said.

"I'm paying," Creelman cut in. "Have something to eat. Apparently, the lamb stew is good. Also the omelet and the lasagna."

It did smell good in the cafe. And it had been a long time since breakfast.

"Meat loaf, please," I said, handing back the menu to the waitress.

Did Creelman just smile? It was fleeting, but I think he did.

"Two orders of meat loaf. Honestly!" she said, shaking her head. "And to drink?"

"Coffee," Creelman said.

"Chocolate milk, please," I ordered.

"Aren't you polite," the waitress said, and she turned to Creelman. "Is this your grandson?"

"He's a volunteer at Twillingate Cemetery," Creelman explained.

"Really?" the waitress said. "But this isn't Wednesday afternoon."

"In between shifts, Derek's a spy," Creelman said.

Embarrassment. I was definitely feeling embarrassment.

"Oh, my," the waitress said, lowering her voice. "Well, I'll be sure not to blow your cover."

She left to take our orders to the kitchen.

"I wasn't spying," I said.

"Not very well, that's for sure," Creelman said.

"I was shopping for a gift for Mother's Day," I insisted.

"So you do have a mother?" Creelman said.

"Yes. That's who I was shopping for."

"I thought you were an orphan."

"An orphan?"

"Orphans like cemeteries. They spend a lot of time searching for their pasts."

"And you think I like cemeteries?"

"You signed up for cemetery duty, didn't you?"

I thought it was best just to shrug. It seemed mean to tell him that cemetery duty was all that was left on account of my pink eye.

"What's with your t-shirt?" Creelman asked, an eyebrow raised.

I looked down at the one I was wearing. It read, *I'm unique. Just like everyone else.*

"I collect sayings," I explained, more sheepishly than I wanted, "and make my own t-shirts."

"Why?"

"I don't know. It's just a hobby, I guess."

"Do you want to be a writer when you grow up or something?"

"Well, I like designing words with pictures, like posters or book covers and whatnot."

"A graphic designer, then?"

"Maybe."

"Have you read any good epitaphs?"

"Epitaphs?"

"Epitaphs. A phrase or a poem about the deceased, carved in stone."

"At the cemetery? No. Not yet."

"I have a book at home. It's a collection of epitaphs called *Famous Last Words*."

I couldn't imagine reading a book like that. How would it go? *Rest in peace. Rest in peace. Rest in peace. Gone but not forgotten. Rest in peace.*

Boring. And nothing I could use for t-shirts, that's for sure.

"Some are pretty funny," said Creelman.

"Funny?" I repeated doubtfully. "Really?"

"My favorite is *I told you I was sick.*"

"On a gravestone?" I laughed. "That would make a good t-shirt to wear if you've got the measles or something."

"Some aren't as funny," Creelman continued, instantly sobering.

"No," I said, trying to keep pace with his changing moods. "I bet they aren't."

He cleared his throat to recite.

"Stranger stop and cast an eye. As you are now, so once was I. As I am now, so you will be. Remember Death and follow me."

"Yikes," I said, shifting in my vinyl seat. It made a grumbling sound.

"Did I show you the epitaph at the cemetery with all the letters carved upside down?"

"No," I said. "Not yet. What happened?"

"Many early carvers couldn't read. They just carved whatever was written out for them. That's why symbols were important. Everyone could read symbols."

"Oh. So the stone carver copied out the words with the paper upside down and didn't notice," I said.

Creelman nodded. Then he stopped nodding.

"*This wasn't my idea,*" he said.

"Pardon me?" I asked.

"That's another funny epitaph in the book. It reads, *This wasn't my idea.*"

"That is funny. *Famous Last Words* sounds like a good book," I admitted.

"There's a copy in the library," Creelman said.

"Maybe I'll sign it out," I said, and I meant it.

"Or you can borrow mine," Creelman offered. His scowl softened.

That caught me off guard. Was Creelman being nice?

"Why are you yawning?" he demanded, scowl returning full-force.

"Am I?" I said, yawning. "I guess I'm tired."

"I'm tired, too," Creelman said. "That's because I'm old. What's the matter with you?"

"I didn't get a good sleep last night."

"Why not?"

I shifted in my seat again. More grumbling sounds. I didn't like where this conversation was headed.

"I had a nightmare," I admitted.

Where was the waitress with our food?

"A nightmare? What about?"

"A cemetery."

"A *cemetery!*" Creelman scoffed. "Don't tell me you think there are ghosts, etcetera, at the cemetery!"

"No! It's not like that at all," I insisted.

"Good. Because there are no ghosts, just so you know."

"I know that," I said. I could feel my cheeks burning.

"No ghosts. No vampires. No zombies."

"Yes, I know."

"No phantoms. No ghouls. No werewolves."

"Right," I said, but I wondered if he might change his mind after spending more time with Merrilee.

Creelman scowled at me for a full minute while I stared at the swinging doors to the kitchen, willing the waitress to reappear.

No luck. I looked back at Creelman.

"Still. People can be haunted," he admitted, his face softening again.

"What do you mean? You just said there are no ghosts."

"People can be troubled by past events. They're haunted because of things not resolved."

"Things not resolved?" I repeated.

"Here we are," the waitress said, doors swinging in her wake. She set down our beverages, then moved to the next table.

I took a long drink of chocolate milk through my straw.

Creelman was wrong. Sure, what happened to Dennis bothered me. It bothered me practically every night. But there was nothing to resolve. I knew perfectly well how that terrible story ended.

Creelman stirred a big dollop of cream into his coffee and poured in the sugar. He set his spoon down.

"So, what's haunting you?" he asked, raising his mug to his mouth.

I don't know if it was because of the friendly waitress, or the tasty smells in the cafe, or the fact that I had been caught spying on Creelman, but I felt a confession welling from deep inside. My garage door started to roll open, letting a shaft of sunlight stretch across the unswept cement floor.

In an unexpected rush of words, I blurted, "There was an accident."

"When?" Creelman asked.

"I was only little," I answered.

"What happened?"

"We were playing. Me and a friend."

"Playing?" Creelman repeated.

"My friend had an orange rubber ball."

"I see," Creelman said. He took a slow sip of coffee.

And then Creelman disappeared, because in my mind's eye, I heaved my garage door wide open and light shone into all four corners. Then I found myself back in Ferndale on the lawn at our house with the new trees, a fresh popsicle stick in my pocket and the lawnmower whining in the backyard. I described the scene.

"It's hot out. Everyone else is inside. The ball is fun. My friend kicks it to me. I miss. I keep missing. So does he. The ball is going everywhere. It's tricky."

"Where are your parents?" came a voice.

"Dad's cutting the lawn in the backyard. The mower is noisy. Mom is inside lying on the couch. Her head hurts because of the heat. She has a bag of ice cubes around her neck.

"But I have my friend to play with. I like him. He has a big collection of trucks and tractors in his backyard sandbox. They can dig and scoop. Once he let me take his dump truck home to play with, and I filled it with my whole marble collection.

"Right now, we have the orange rubber ball. I miss again. It rolls under a bush by our front steps. When I crawl underneath to get it, I bump the scab on my knee and it starts bleeding. When I stand, bits of freshly cut grass are sticking to my legs. I pat down my pocket to make sure I still have the popsicle stick. I think about my plastic horses and the corral I am going to build.

"'You missed!' my friend calls out between laughs. 'You missed! You missed!'

"'I can't see,' I yell back. 'The sun's in the way.'

"It is so hot out. There is no shade. The sun is coming down, and it is right in my face whenever I look over to where my friend is.

"'Kick it,' he yells. 'Kick it. It's my turn.'

"I put the orange ball down in front of me. The grass smells sweet. I stand back. Then I take a run at the ball and kick it as hard as I can.

"Bam! Perfect hit! It soars over my lawn and my

friend's lawn, too. It soars over the sidewalk. It soars onto the street.

"'I'll get it!' he yells. He's laughing.

"I look for him, but the sun is still in the way. He turns to chase the ball, and now the sun is in his way, too. And because of the lawnmower, he doesn't hear the car.

"My friend runs.

"Brakes squeal.

"He flies backwards into the air, his arms reaching out to the car that has just hit him, his legs dangling. He crumples to the ground.

"I hear sounds of a car door opening.

"Cries for help.

"The lawnmower stops.

"Screen doors creak open along both sides of my street.

"What is happening?

"I make myself walk toward the empty car. My legs do not work well. My friend is lying near the curb. His eyes are open, but he is not moving. His head is in a puddle of blood. The puddle spreads. So much blood.

"Someone pushes me aside as she rushes by.

"His mom.

"Then my dad.

"Now a crowd surrounds my friend.

"A man I do not know sits all alone on our lawn. He groans as he rocks back and forth, his head in his hands.

"I hear sirens.

"'Derek!'

"It is my mom.

"'I'm here. I'm here. I'm here.'

"She keeps saying this and she hugs me hard. I cannot move. I cannot breathe. She carries me inside.

"I throw up. My popsicle is all over my shirt. It sticks to me. She cleans me up, and I tell her that I'm cold. She wraps me in a blanket and lays me down on the couch.

"'I'm here,' she tells me again and again, but she is crying."

"Two meat loaves," our waitress chirped, sliding identical plates of meat with gravy, mashed potatoes and peas in front of Creelman and me.

My living room dissolved and I was back in the cafe.

Creelman and I ate in silence. When his plate was almost empty, he took a big gulp of coffee, then asked, "Did you go to the funeral?"

I nodded with my mouth full. I don't remember much about what happened in the days that followed the accident. But I can still smell the flowers, I can hear the choir music, and I can touch a lamb carved out of stone. In my mind, the stone is always cold, even in the summer.

I finished my meat loaf and set down my fork. I placed my hands on my lap and was surprised by how steady they were. Normally, I would be shaking or sweating or both, having told the story to the very end. I folded my napkin and glanced at Creelman.

Creelman had abandoned his meal and was staring intently out the window toward the cemetery, as if he had forgotten that I was even there. He slowly drummed his fingers on the table, balling up a napkin in his other hand.

"Need a top-up?" the waitress asked when she came by with a pot of coffee.

Creelman didn't seem to hear her. He continued to stare in the direction of the cemetery, lost in his own thoughts.

She hesitated, glanced at me, then filled his cup.

"Give him a minute," she said softly to me. "He always comes back."

Where does he go, I wanted to ask.

It was then that I was certain he had a secret, too.

We sat for several more minutes like that, him staring out the window at the cemetery, me wondering if I would ever get a good night's sleep again.

"Do you recall anything else?" Creelman finally asked when the waitress came by with the bill.

I thought back and quietly poked around my mind's garage, its door still wide open to passersby. Were there any details left to discover? Then it came to me.

"I remember going to bed early the night of the accident. It was still light out. I could hear police officers talking to my parents in the living room, but I couldn't make out their words. The fan in my room blew hot sticky air as I tossed and tossed. And then I woke up in the middle of the night. I crept out of my bedroom and unlocked the front door. It was eerie dark, but still warm. And quiet. I walked across our front yard to the street. Then I walked up and down the street under the burning lampposts that collected moths and hummed."

"Why do you think you did that?" Creelman asked.

"I was looking for my friend. I walked and walked and only stopped when I came across the exact spot where he was hit."

"How did you know?"

"The bloodstain."

Creelman rubbed his face and took another drink of coffee.

I thought back some more.

"It rained hard the next day, but the bloodstain never went away. Every time I came out of our house, I spotted it, and it froze me in my tracks. I finally said something to my mom, but she told me that she couldn't see anything. I led her by the hand to the spot. I knelt right beside the stain and pointed. 'Look,' I said. 'It's right here.'"

"She just sadly shook her head.

"'You'll be okay' was all she would say every time I brought it up. After a while, I didn't talk about the stain, but I wouldn't go out the front door anymore. I would only go in and out of the house through the back door and down the alley. I never played in the front yard again."

"And then what happened?" Creelman asked.

"We moved away," I said. "We moved here for a fresh start."

Creelman set down his mug. He took his time with his next question.

"Derek. If you went back there now, to the street where the accident happened, what do you think you'd see?"

"The bloodstain. It's still there. I'm sure of it."

Six

———

Rubbings

WHEN I MET PASCAL and Merrilee the next week at
the cemetery, I decided that I wouldn't mention my
lunch with Creelman. They would be full of questions,
and because Creelman and I talked mostly about the
accident, there wasn't much to report other than that.
Besides, my nightmares had become a regular event,
and I was really tired of thinking about it.

"I've asked everyone I know about Trevor Tower,"
Pascal said as soon as I arrived. "Nobody's heard of
him."

"It's all very strange," Merrilee agreed, crossing her
arms in her red plastic bunnies-and-carrots jacket.

"A dead end," I added, enjoying saying it at the cemetery gate.

"You wish!" Merrilee snapped.

She had no sense of humor whatsoever, despite the
bunnies jacket.

"Then what's our next move?" I asked, still not convinced that tracking down a complete stranger and rummaging through his locker filled with secrets — if that's what the codes in the mystery books meant us to do — was even remotely a good idea.

Merrilee scanned the cemetery, as if looking for an answer among the silent gravestones.

"We already know he's not buried here," Pascal said.

"I know that," Merrilee replied, fixing her gaze in the direction of the new section of the cemetery.

I looked at Pascal and he looked at me. Is this when Merrilee would finally transform into a zombie or something?

But no. Merrilee stayed Merrilee.

"What's wrong?" Pascal pressed, eyeing her suspiciously and taking a step closer to me.

"Nothing," Merrilee said, still staring at the new section with the precisely lined-up granite markers. "Just a feeling." Her voice trailed off.

Again, Pascal looked at me and I looked at Pascal. Then I gave him a quick nod, urging him to go ahead and ask.

"Okay, Merrilee. What's with all the spooky talk?" he demanded, taking my cue.

I faced her, too, glad that one of us had finally spoken up.

"What do you mean?" she asked.

"Spooky talk," Pascal repeated. He held his hands up

and waved them in the air like a hovering ghost.

"And you actually *like* being in a cemetery," I added.

"You two find me spooky?" she asked, pushing her glasses up on her nose.

Awkward silence.

"Do you?"

"Kind of," we each muttered, me scuffing at the lumpy ground.

"Well good. That's what I was going for," she said brightly.

Merrilee set her knapsack down and calmly unzipped it.

I held my breath, expecting a colony of vampire bats to fly out, but no. She took out a library book instead and sat down with her back against the iron gate, dismissing both of us.

But I wasn't about to be dismissed so easily. Not again.

"What are you reading now?" I asked.

"Another mystery book."

"I thought we'd solved the last mystery book code," I said, interrupting her some more.

"We did. But I've discovered that I like mystery novels, with or without a code."

She paused.

"Does that also make me spooky?"

"No," I admitted, realizing that I wouldn't mind reading another mystery, just for the challenge of solving it. "Hey. Maybe I should make you a t-shirt that says, *If reading's no fun, you're doing it wrong.*

"Good one," she said flatly.

She opened to where she had inserted her bookmark — the playing card with the Queen of Spades wearing a hand-drawn pair of glasses.

"Where'd you get the card?" Pascal said, joining me in my game to keep her from her book.

"I found it in a paperback I bought at a used book store. It's one of my favorite discoveries. I've been using it ever since." She didn't look up from her book as she spoke, but her attempts to ignore us were futile.

"Did you draw on the glasses?" I asked pleasantly.

"No," she said, pushing up her own pair on her nose. "Someone else did. That's why I like it so much. It speaks to me."

Pascal mouthed the word *spooky* to me while she turned a page.

"Aren't you worried that you'll forget to take it out when you return the book to the library?" I asked.

"I might. But I know exactly where it would end up," she said, refusing to take her eyes off her book.

"Are you telling us that you can see into the future?" Pascal asked, elbowing me.

"Sadly, no."

"But you just said ..."

Merrilee cut Pascal off with a heavy sigh. She gave each of us a withering look.

"It would end up on Loyola's bulletin board at the library. Haven't you seen it?"

Pascal and I shook our heads.

"She collects things that people have left tucked in library books and has a display of them behind her desk."

"What kind of things?" I asked.

"You'd be surprised what people will use as bookmarks. Lottery tickets, love letters, greeting cards, travel tickets, old photographs, sketches, grocery lists, newspaper clippings, unpublished poetry, pressed four-leaf clovers."

"I just fold the corner of the page to mark where I am," Pascal admitted.

"Pascal!" I said. "What if everyone did that?"

"No problem," he said. "They'd just have to remember to unfold the corner when they're done. Like I do."

I gave up and turned to Merrilee.

"What's the most interesting item Loyola has found?" I asked.

Merrilee sighed again and closed her book. "Her favorite bookmark is a supply list for an expedition to a monastery in India. It's written with a fountain pen on a type of paper that's no longer made."

"Here comes the Brigade," Pascal announced.

Merrilee got to her feet, and we watched as Creelman, flanked by Wooster and Preeble, crossed the street. They made their way directly to the cemetery gate. This time each of them carried a plastic blue bin. They set the lidded bins down in front of us.

"Good afternoon," Creelman said. "Today's lesson: rubbings."

"Rubbings," Pascal predictably repeated before the Brigade could catch their breath. "What's that?"

Wooster and Preeble crossed their arms and took a step back.

"Ever put a leaf or a penny underneath a piece of paper and rub a crayon on top of the paper so that you get an image? That's a rubbing," Creelman explained.

"I did that once, only I drew a picture in crayon, covered it in black paint, then scratched out a drawing so that the colors underneath showed through."

"Not the same thing," said Creelman, turning away from Pascal. "Now, inside each of these bins you'll find a package of jumbo crayons, scissors, masking tape and nonfusible interfacing fabric."

Pascal took a few steps so that he planted himself directly in front of Creelman again.

"Reusable what?" he asked.

"*Nonfusible* interfacing fabric. You buy it at fabric stores to stiffen collars and buttonholes and cuffs. But that's not important. We use it here because it doesn't tear as easily as paper."

Pascal was about to ask another question, but Creelman gave a dismissive wave of his hand.

"Now, open your bins."

We did. Inside my bin was a roll of white fabric and all the other items Creelman had listed. Except mine also had one more item — Creelman's book of epitaphs called *Famous Last Words*.

I glanced up at Creelman, but he didn't look my way.

"What you're going to do is select a gravestone that you like. Just make sure that the stone you select is in good shape, that it isn't cracking or weakened in any way. Then you need to cut off a piece of interfacing that is larger than the stone you want to rub."

"So we can pick any stone we want? Any stone at all?" Pascal asked, with a sweep of his hand that covered the entire cemetery.

"No," Creelman replied. He turned to me. "Derek, which stones are good for rubbing?"

"Ones that are not cracked or weakened in any way."

Creelman nodded curtly. I could see that he was going to treat me as if he still didn't know much about me or my past. I was so relieved that I didn't mind being singled out for questions.

"Got it," Pascal said, undaunted as usual.

He began to wander off with his bin in search of a gravestone.

"Wait!" Creelman barked. "I'm not done."

Pascal trailed back to us, clumsily dropping his bin to the ground.

"As I was saying, pick a stone, a stone that is not cracked or weakened, and cut a piece of interfacing larger than the stone. Tape the interfacing dead center over the area you want to rub. Pick a color of crayon you like and peel off the paper covering the crayon. Then rub with the side of the crayon — not the tip! — against the interfacing, and watch the image appear. If you do this correctly, your rubbing will be an exact replica of the stone. When you get home, use an iron to set the crayon into the fabric. Then you'll have an artifact that is suitable for framing."

I glanced at Merrilee, who was listening intently to Creelman's every word. This kind of project was right up her alley.

"When you say *iron*," Merrilee probed, "how exactly do you do that?"

"Place your rubbing face-up on your ironing board with an old towel over it. Then with a hot iron, press down on the towel. This will melt the rubbing beneath it into the interfacing fabric so that you have a permanent image."

Merrilee nodded along with Creelman's instructions. I had never seen her look so fascinated, so eager. I was certain that her bedroom walls would soon be covered in spooky rubbings of every type of skull and crossbones imaginable.

I wished she'd turn into a vampire and get it over with. What was she waiting for?

Creelman seemed to pick up on Merrilee's enthusiasm.

"If you ever want to do a rubbing at another cemetery, be sure to get permission first," he added. "Not all cemeteries allow it."

We nodded.

"That's it for now," Creelman said. "Pick your gravestone and begin. And be careful. We don't want to see any crayon wax on any gravestone. We'll be back later to check your work."

The Brigade left without a backward glance, leaving us behind with our blue bins.

I turned to face Pascal and Merrilee, but Merrilee was already off like a shot.

"So much to choose from," Pascal said. "What do you think you'll pick? One with an hourglass? An angel? A weeping willow?"

"I think I'm going to look for one with an interesting epitaph," I said, thinking back to my conversation with Creelman. "There's bound to be something I like that's been written in stone."

"Okay. Well, good luck," Pascal said, and he wandered away with his bin.

I picked up mine and headed in the opposite direction. I slowly made my way up and down the rows, reading the gravestones one by one.

Rest in peace.
Rest in peace.
Rest in peace.

The oldest ones were more of the same, so I made

my way over to the north section, past the marbles. There I read some interesting epitaphs with more modern phrases. Then I came across a great one carved underneath the person's date of birth and death. It read, *Writer. End of Story.*

I set my bin down and opened the lid. I took my time and followed Creelman's instructions exactly. I didn't want to mess up, especially because he had lent me his book without a word.

I carefully rubbed across the epitaph with a blue crayon and the letters came through boldly. The sun was warm on my back, the ground was drying out, and the grass was soft and bright green — signs of spring. When I was almost done, I stood to see where Merrilee and Pascal were working.

Merrilee had remained in the oldest part of the cemetery, near poor Enoch's plot where there were plenty of skulls and crossbones to choose from. No surprise there.

Pascal had moved to the marble section of the cemetery, just before the first hedgerow.

Except for an older couple who were visiting a gravestone a few rows ahead of me, I had the granite section to myself.

I was just finishing up when the couple came over to see what I was doing. They looked to be the same age as my grandparents and were dressed as if they had just come from church.

"What do you have there?" the woman asked kindly.

"I'm taking a rubbing of this gravestone."

"Did you know this person?"

"No, but I like the epitaph."

"*Writer. End of story.* Oh, that is clever. Lenore was always very funny."

I reread the name on the gravestone. *Lenore Swinimer.*

"You knew her?" I asked.

"We knew of her," the man said. "She wrote a column for a coastal magazine that we liked to read. Do you go to school around here?"

The woman quickly turned to him.

"Stop your questions. You're retired now, remember!"

"Once a school superintendent, always a school superintendent," he said with a shrug, but then he fixed a stare on me, still expecting an answer.

I was pretty sure that school superintendents kept records of attendance and dealt with kids who skipped class.

"I go to Queensview Elementary," I explained quickly. "The grade sixes do community work on Wednesday afternoons for the last three months of the school year. I ended up with cemetery duty."

"How wonderful! We were just visiting Mother," the woman said, nodding toward the row they had just come from. I could see that they had left flowers on top of one of the gravestones.

"Oh," I said. I was at a dead loss about what more to say. This was the first time I had talked to people who actually knew someone buried in the cemetery.

"I'm sorry," I added hesitantly.

"That's okay. She died years ago. This is the anniversary of her passing."

"Oh," I said.

"It's a beautiful day," she remarked, holding her face up to the sun.

The man stood with his hands on his hips and surveyed the rest of the cemetery.

"Nothing like a cemetery to teach us about local history. They keep great records."

I thought back to how quickly Creelman was able to check to see if Trevor Tower was buried at Twillingate. I nodded in agreement.

"Cemeteries. Churches. Schools. They all keep great records," the man continued.

Great records? *That* got me thinking! We could find out if Trevor Tower had been a student at Queensview by checking the school's records!

Simple!

"Do schools keep records of every student who ever attended?" I asked, just to be sure.

"Guaranteed," the man said.

Trevor Tower. If he had been a student at Queensview, then it would be easy enough to confirm just by asking the secretary at the school's office. Had Merrilee or Pascal thought of that? No, I was certain they hadn't.

"Well, we must be on our way," the woman said.

"Yes, we should if we still want to stop for lunch," the man said, checking his watch.

"Are you going to Sacred Grounds Cafe?" I asked.

"We might," the man said. "It's close."

"If you do," I said, "try the meat loaf. It's excellent."

"Thanks for the tip," the man said.

The couple headed off.

I packed up my bin and put Creelman's book and my rubbing into my knapsack.

The next day during recess, I stood in the hallway outside of the school's office and waited to meet Pascal and Merrilee. They arrived together.

"What's the plan?" Pascal asked. "You're going to ask the secretary if Trevor Tower was a student here? Just like that?"

"Sure," I said. "Why not?"

"She's going to ask why we want to know," Merrilee warned.

"So we'll tell her," I said.

"Tell her what, exactly?" Merrilee asked.

"We'll tell her that we found a book at the public library with his name in it, and we wondered if he had been a student here. That's the truth, more or less. We don't have to say that his name was written in a secret code."

Pascal and Merrilee thought this over.

"I guess we could say that," Merrilee said at last.

"Let's do it," Pascal added.

Together, we filed into the office. Ms. Albright, the school's secretary, was at her desk talking on the telephone. When she hung up, she surveyed the three of us, then settled on Merrilee.

"Merrilee! Have you been sent to see the principal? *Again*?"

"No," Merrilee shot back with surprising force.

"I'm very glad to hear it," Ms. Albright said. "You and the principal must be running out of things to talk about."

Merrilee said nothing, but she gave me an angry little push forward.

"We were wondering if you could check the school records for us," I said in my politest voice. "We'd like to know if Trevor Tower was ever a student here."

"Trevor Tower?"

"Yes. Trevor Tower. Could you please check?"

"Trevor Tower? What do you know about Trevor Tower?"

"Nothing. Not a thing."

"Nothing?"

"No."

"Trevor Tower. It's the same thing every year. I don't get it."

"What do you mean?" I asked.

"Every year, a student comes by to ask me about Trevor Tower."

"Is that right?" I said. I realized then that the mystery book codes had to have been floating around in the public library for years, and that others had been on the same trail before us.

"So you've already looked him up?" I asked. "You keep good records?"

"I most certainly do," Ms. Albright said.

I thought of my list of t-shirt sayings. If I were to make one for Ms. Albright, it would read, *Not here to make friends.*

The telephone rang.

"Good afternoon. This is Queensview Elementary. How may I help you?"

I formed a tight huddle with Pascal and Merrilee.

"I don't think she's going to tell us. She's too suspicious," Merrilee whispered.

"Well, what do you want me to do?"

"We'll have to trick her into answering our question. Come at her from the side."

"Come at her from the side? What's that supposed to mean?" I whispered.

"Follow my lead," Merrilee whispered. "And you," she added, turning to Pascal, "you say nothing."

Pascal opened his mouth to object, but Ms. Albright hung up the telephone. Before she could say anything further, Merrilee jumped in.

"We're really enjoying cemetery duty," Merrilee announced.

"I'm glad," Ms. Albright said. "Community service is important. Is Mr. Creelman still with the Brigade?"

"Yes, he is," Merrilee said. "I think he's been there since the beginning of time."

Ms. Albright chuckled. "You might be right. But I hear that he's been having some health issues, so I wondered if he was still keeping up with his volunteer work."

"Well, he sure knows everything there is to know about that cemetery. Parts of a grave marker. Types of stones. How to clean them. And just yesterday, we learned how to make rubbings."

"That sounds lovely," Ms. Albright said, as she began to straighten the paperwork on her desk.

We were losing her. I looked anxiously at Merrilee.

But Merrilee was unflappable.

"Mr. Creelman even knows who is buried in every single plot. The cemetery keeps amazing records."

"Is that so?" Ms. Albright said, reloading her stapler.

"You can give him a name, and just like that, he can tell you if that person is buried at the cemetery or not."

"Well, good for him," Ms. Albright said, putting stray pencils into her pencil holder.

"It's impressive," Merrilee agreed. "We asked Mr. Creelman about Trevor Tower," she added sadly. "He looked up Trevor's name for us, but there was no record."

"Oh, my! Trevor would be far too young for the cemetery, I should hope. And besides, he and his family moved away years ago, right after Trevor graduated from grade six," Ms. Albright said, dumping holes from her hole puncher into her wastebasket like confetti, without realizing she had confirmed that Trevor *had* been a student at Queensview.

"Moved away?" I repeated.

To tell the truth, I was a bit relieved. If Trevor no longer lived in our town, and those mystery code books had been floating around the library for years and years, then there was no longer any locker to open. We had reached the ultimate dead end and could now move on with our lives.

"With all the student records you take care of, how can you be so certain about Trevor?" Merrilee asked.

"It's easy to remember the names of the students chosen to participate in the school's time-capsule program. That only happens once every seven years."

"Trevor was selected?" Merrilee asked, elbowing me ever so slightly.

"Yes. Seven years ago. That's why it's easy to remember him."

Pascal gasped, but Ms. Albright didn't seem to notice.

"So, his locker is a time capsule," I said, almost in a whisper. "It's still here."

"That's right. Locked up and scheduled to be opened forty-three years from now."

Her words, so casually dropped, almost knocked me to my knees. But Merrilee took a bold step forward and leaned her hands on Ms. Albright's tidied desk.

"Where is it?" she demanded.

Seven

———

Famous Last Words

"What luck! Trevor has a time-capsule locker!" Pascal said in awe as we hurried along the upstairs hallway, our shoes squeaking against the linoleum. "And there it is! I can see the plaque from here."

We stopped and stood in front of Trevor Tower's locker. The engraved metal plaque fixed to it gave Trevor Tower's name, the year he graduated and the year that the locker was to be reopened. Except for the plaque, the locker seemed ordinary in every other way.

"Look," Merrilee said.

She pointed to the lock securing Trevor's time capsule, which was also ordinary, but I could see why she was excited. It was not a lock that needed a key. It was a combination lock with a dial.

"Twenty-eight. Thirty-four. Eighteen. That has to be the combination," she said.

The three of us spied left and right, but the hallway was crowded with lunchtime traffic. Even worse, Trevor's locker was located directly across from the school's music room, which was also used as a homework drop-in center over lunch. From where we stood, it felt like the busiest part of the school.

"This is no good," I cautioned. "Too many people."

"I can see that," Merrilee said irritably.

"So we're not going to open it today?" Pascal said with disappointment.

"We need to be careful," Merrilee said. "Besides, the locker isn't going anywhere."

"She's right," I said, a bit relieved that we had put off the deed, at least for now.

I was still not convinced that breaking into a time capsule filled with secrets and meant to stay locked for fifty years was a good idea.

And yet, I had to admit that I was now a little bit intrigued about what the contents might be. Secrets, we knew that, but what kind?

I thought back to my lunch with Creelman and about how, for the first time ever, I had kept my mind's garage door open and had taken a really good look around. Up until then, I had always been afraid of what I might find lurking in the shadowy corners. But with Creelman, I had remembered all the details of the accident, every last one of them. And although I was still having nightmares, at least I had confronted the facts I knew about that terrible day. Doing so somehow made me feel safer and more in control.

If I could live through telling Creelman everything I knew about the accident, I was sure that whatever was inside Trevor Tower's locker could not be as big an ordeal as I had imagined.

"We should complete a week of observations," Merrilee advised. "Each of us will make notes about what's happening in this hallway at various times throughout the day, and then we'll compare notes. That way we'll be able to pick the quietest time to break in."

"What do you think is in there?" Pascal asked. He took a bold step forward and sniffed. "It doesn't smell."

"Step away from that locker!" Merrilee whispered harshly. "We don't want to cause any suspicion. Everyone, walk away. We've never had this conversation."

She turned on her heels and marched down the hallway, back the way we had come.

Pascal and I shrugged, then headed to our classroom.

It was threatening rain when we showed up for cemetery duty the next Wednesday afternoon. The dark clouds hung low, and in the distance, lightning struck. The first plops of rain hit the grave markers surrounding us.

"I bet we'll be in the library today," I predicted, as the three of us stood waiting by the gate.

Sure enough, Loyola whistled from the front steps of

the library, the hood of her sweatshirt pulled over her head to protect against the weather.

"The Brigade's in here," she yelled, hastily waving us over.

We left the cemetery, but I fell behind when I stopped to look left, right, left, and then left, right and left again before crossing the street. I caught up to the others on the library stairs. They still hadn't noticed my extra-cautious habit of checking for traffic.

Once inside, we made our way past the stacks to the research area at the back of the library. The Brigade were already sitting at the tables when we arrived. They were leafing through piles of books they had collected. Three blue plastic bins were stacked on the floor beside Creelman.

We slid into some seats across from them.

"Today's lesson is going to build on what you already know about symbolism and how epitaphs have changed over time. To do that, you'll be designing your own gravestone," Creelman announced.

"Now we're talking!" Pascal exclaimed. He reached for a blue bin.

I was also excited. Design work was something I could always throw myself into. Words combined with pictures and whatnot! I nearly whooped!

"Not yet," Creelman said, glowering at Pascal. He moved the bin out of Pascal's reach with a push of his foot.

Pascal settled back in his chair.

The rain had picked up force and was now spraying against the stained glass. We had escaped indoors just in time.

"In order to design your own gravestone, you'll need to do some research. Find out what other cultures and religions like to put on their grave markers so that you can make informed choices. For example, there are specific ways that the military respect their fallen soldiers. And there are specific occupations like ship-building and fire-fighting that have their own emblems."

"Emblems? You mean songs? How do you put songs on a gravestone?" Pascal asked.

"What's that, now?" Creelman asked, his scowl deepening if that was possible.

"He's confusing *emblem* with *anthem*," Merrilee jumped in. She turned to Pascal. "An emblem is like a crest or a coat of arms. An anthem is what you sing before hockey games."

"Got it," Pascal said. He faced Creelman, waiting to pounce with another question.

Creelman cleared his throat and continued at his steady pace, but started fiddling with a pencil. It looked like he was desperate for a cigarette.

"Our earliest gravestones used to be about warning the rest of us that death was certain or that time on earth was fleeting. *Here lies the body of …* with pictures of coffins or crossbones or shovels. Not very cheery.

Then attitudes changed, and gravestones started to include symbols of hope and life after death. Lots of winged cherubs. The dead were thought to be asleep. Later, gravestones featured urns and weeping willow trees, which were symbols for the grievers who were left behind, and not so much about the dead. Nowadays, you'll see gravestones that tell us something about who the buried person was. Symbols include hobbies or pets or whatever else that person held special in life."

"Maybe I'll include symbols of my favorite band or what I like to eat," Pascal said.

Creelman did not respond to Pascal directly, but he did not pound on the table either, even though he looked as if he might have wanted to. Instead, he plowed on with his directions.

"Remember, a gravestone, through words and art, tells the world who you were and how you want to be remembered. Most important, keep this in mind. Your choices are permanent." He pounded the table. "*Per-man-ent!* They're etched in stone. You can't change a gravestone like you can change a t-shirt," Creelman warned, and he gave me a level stare.

I looked down at the t-shirt I was wearing that day. It read, *If you don't make mistakes, you're not really try-ing.*

"So, look through these books before you begin. And when you're ready, take one of the bins. Inside you'll find a large roll of paper, felt markers and colored pencils. There's tracing paper if you want to copy a design from a book, and glue and scissors. You'll also find alphabet stencils so that you can write out your epitaph."

Creelman turned to me and his face softened. I almost didn't recognize him, except that he had had that same look when he was staring out the window back in the cafe.

"Give careful thought to your epitaph. These will be your famous last words. You need to choose something that will withstand the ravages of time."

A dark silence rolled in like a fog, and when I glanced again at Creelman, he was busy rearranging his face into his usual scowl.

"We'll be back to check your work."

And to no one's surprise, the Brigade marched out of the library into the downpour.

As I watched them leave, I thought back to the book of epitaphs that Creelman had lent me. I had been reading it every night, mostly when I woke up from my nightmares. I had come across a few sayings that would be great for my t-shirt collection, and I remembered one epitaph in particular that I thought I wouldn't mind seeing on my own gravestone.

Still, I had no idea about the symbols that I might like to use. I reached for the nearest pile and began to leaf through one of the books.

"I'm looking for joyful symbols," Merrilee remarked

as she flipped through the pages of her chosen book. "I want mine to be about celebrating life."

Joyful symbols? Good grief! I was dead certain she would go for all the spooky ones to create a truly terrifying gravestone that would force people to take a wide circle as they passed by. But I didn't say a word. I realized that I was never going to figure out Merrilee, and I wasn't about to die trying.

"I'm going to go for a superstar theme," Pascal said. "When people walk by my gravestone, they'll wish they had known me, and weep. What about you, Derek?"

"I think I'd like mine to be peaceful. I'd like to make people feel comforted."

Merrilee stopped flipping pages. She looked directly at me with an intense stare.

"That's really nice," she said, but with no emotion whatsoever.

Then she went back to her books as if she had said nothing at all.

Was she being pleasant or spooky? It was baffling. I went back to my books.

As I flipped through the pages, I realized that there were symbols for absolutely everything imaginable. It turned out that if I wanted to go with peace and comfort, my symbol choices included a dove, a lighthouse and an anchor.

That was a nice discovery because those symbols reminded me of the yellow and blue cottage we rented every summer for our family vacation. It came with a small two-person sailboat, and my dad had spent hours teaching me the ropes. I loved the feel of the wind pushing the sails, and how we could skim across the water so quickly. I loved the quietness of it all, and the excitement during gusts. I loved the musty smell of the life jackets and the cool spray on my face and the peanut butter and jam sandwiches my dad packed, which we ate when we reached the island with the lighthouse.

I grabbed a blue bin and opened it to take out the supplies. I wasn't sure how much time passed, but I was pleased with how my design was coming together. It was the same feeling that I got with the t-shirts I made.

The three of us worked in silence. The only sound was the rain sweeping across the stained-glass windows. I thought back to our first day of cemetery duty, and I remembered how creeped-out I had been back then.

What had changed? It surprised me to realize that I had actually begun to look forward to Wednesday afternoons. Merrilee was right. It was nice to be working outdoors. And Pascal turned out to be pretty entertaining, sometimes asking questions that I would never dare to ask. The three of us did not have much in common, but here we were, working together, getting along.

I sat back and surveyed the pile of books on the table.

Could Creelman also have helped to make me feel

better about cemeteries? Were his weekly lectures somehow lessening my fear of graveyards? And then I thought about it — reading weathered marble, figuring out carved symbols, mapping plots, cleaning stones, taking rubbings of epitaphs that we liked. Creelman had been showing us all along that cemeteries were much more about the living than they were about the dead.

"Done," Merrilee announced.

She stood up to admire her drawing. Pascal and I joined her.

Merrilee's gravestone featured a large harp surrounded by a wreath of acorns. Below that, two winged angels knelt facing each other while drinking tea. Her epitaph read, *Life is for the living.*

"Nice," both Pascal and I said at the same time, and I realized that Merrilee had also been taking in Creelman's message.

Pascal and I continued to work on our gravestones while Merrilee disappeared among the stacks, then made her way to the library's front desk to talk to Loyola about the latest book she had read. Her voice and Loyola's booming laughter wafted back to where we sat.

As I colored in my lighthouse, my mind wandered.

A popsicle. The sound of a lawnmower. An orange rubber ball.

    The smell of grass. The sun. Laughter.

Dennis. The stained pavement. A carved stone lamb.

"Derek?"

I looked up.

"You okay?" Pascal asked.

It took a few seconds to realize where I was. I looked at my work. I had been coloring the beacon of the lighthouse for who knows how long.

"Sure," I said, trying to look casual by stretching my arms. "I'm going to get a drink of water."

I made my way to the fountain by the front desk and took a long cool drink.

"Hey, Derek," Merrilee said when she spotted me. "Come check this out."

She was pointing to Loyola's bulletin board of lost-and-found bookmarks. How many people came back for their lost items, I wondered. Not many judging from the way the items were cluttered and spilling over the sides.

Then I spotted a folded piece of paper with Loyola's name on it.

"What's that?" I asked, pointing to the paper.

Loyola unpinned and unfolded the paper. It had been the front cover of an essay she had written. She read the title out loud.

"'How I Did Not Spend My Summer Vacation.'"

I noted that the fold marks had almost worn through.

I could also see that someone had written a comment underneath the title, but I couldn't read it upside down.

"What does it say?" I asked.

Loyola cleared her throat, blushing slightly.

"*Loyola, you are a gifted storyteller. Promise me that you'll keep writing.*"

"Nice comment," I said. "Is it from a teacher?"

"Yes, back when I was in grade six at Queensview. The teacher was only there for a year, but he was the best one I ever had. I folded the cover into a bookmark and used it for years, until I almost wore it out. Now I just keep it posted here for safekeeping." She folded and pinned the cover to her bulletin board.

"So, are you still writing?" I asked.

"I try, but with all my studying and part-time work here, I only have time to write in the margins, so to speak."

I looked again at the bookmark she had re-pinned to the bulletin board. I studied the frayed fold marks.

"How many years ago were you at Queensview?" I asked, following a hunch.

"Let's see. Seven."

"Seven?"

I remembered what Ms. Albright told us. Trevor Tower sealed his time capsule seven years ago.

Seven years ago exactly.

"Then you must have known Trevor Tower."

"Trevor Tower? Sure, I knew Trevor. But his family moved away right after grade six."

I could feel Merrilee stiffen beside me.

"What can you tell us about him?" I asked. I could not believe my luck.

"Let me think. He loved bulldogs. He liked to fly kites. His parents were pilots, so he moved a lot. Oh, and his locker was chosen for the school's time-capsule program."

I stepped forward in excitement for my next question, but Merrilee secretly tugged the back of my shirt.

I halted and looked at Merrilee, confused.

"We should let Loyola get back to work," she said, dead calm. "We don't want to get her into *trouble*."

"I'm done!" Pascal called from the back of the library.

We turned to see him waving us over to the table where he had been working.

We headed back.

"Why don't you want Loyola to know about the secret codes?" I whispered just before we rejoined Pascal.

"No reason," she said, "other than she's practically a grown-up. And grown-ups always try to interfere whenever kids are trying to solve a mystery. Don't you read?"

"You don't trust her?" I asked, ignoring the insult, which I knew she threw out to try to distract me.

"I don't even trust you," she replied, but she smiled when she said it.

We stopped to admire Pascal's gravestone, which he held up for better viewing. It featured a theater stage with tasseled curtains opening on each side and a string of star-shaped lights across the top. On stage, a lion stood on its hind legs wearing a cape and taking what appeared to be a final bow. Pascal's epitaph read, *No More Encores,* and underneath he had drawn two trumpets that crossed each other.

"Your final performance," Merrilee said.

"Very Hollywood," I said.

"Exactly," Pascal said proudly.

"Loyola knew Trevor Tower," I blurted to Pascal. "They were both in the same class back in grade six at Queensview."

"Oh no! You didn't tell Loyola about the secret codes, did you?" Pascal accused. He turned to Merrilee but pointed to me. "Doesn't he read?"

"Don't worry. I pulled him away in time," Merrilee said, and before I could defend myself, she sidled over to my drawing.

"Are you done?" she asked.

"Not quite," I said, picking up my blue colored pencil. "I still have the ocean to fill in."

I got to work while they watched.

I was happy with my design. A lighthouse flanked by two anchors shone a beacon of light toward the open sea. A dove flew away in the same direction as the beacon of light. My epitaph read, *He set his sails against the gales and went wherever he wanted to go.*

"You're pointing to eternity," Merrilee observed. "That's lovely."

"Thanks," I said, pretty sure that she was being sincere, not spooky.

I was even excited to show my work to Creelman.

When the Brigade returned to the library, they were dripping with rain. They silently studied our gravestones, arms clasped behind their backs as if they were cruising through an art gallery on opening night. Then, as usual, Creelman spoke for the three of them, only this time his words made us puff up like peacocks.

"Good job," he announced.

The Brigade turned to go.

"See you next Wednesday," Creelman growled, and they were off.

But we did not see Creelman the next Wednesday.

Instead, the morning after the library, Ms. Albright sent a note to Pascal, Merrilee and me as we sat in class. We left our desks to report to her office.

"Do you think it's about Trevor Tower?" I nervously asked Merrilee and Pascal as we joined each other in the hallway. "Have we done something wrong?"

"We haven't done anything wrong," Merrilee said grimly. "Not yet, anyway."

"Then what's happening?" I asked. "This can't be good."

"No idea," Merrilee said. "Everyone just keep calm."

We walked the rest of the way in silence. The three of us said nothing as we formed a tense line in front of Ms. Albright's desk.

My heart was pounding and my hands were sweating.

"I'm afraid I have some very sad news," she said, removing her glasses and looking into our faces one at a time.

I swallowed as I dared to glance at Merrilee and Pascal.

Trevor Tower. It had to be something about Trevor Tower or his locker.

"It's Mr. Creelman," Ms. Albright continued. "He died at his home last night."

Eight

Time Capsule

I WAS THE FIRST to speak. And I was angry. I could feel my hands clenching.

"What do you mean?" I demanded. "We just saw Mr. Creelman yesterday. In the library. With the Brigade."

"I'm sorry," Ms. Albright said, remaining calm, speaking slowly. Then she quietly added, "Mr. Creelman appears to have had a heart attack."

"See, that's where you're wrong," I argued, louder than before. "He's a smoker. That's bad for his lungs, but he's trying to quit."

"I believe that smoking is also linked to heart attacks," Ms. Albright said softly.

Her words were so hurtful, but she said them in such a kind voice that she confused me. It made me even more angry.

"What am I supposed to do with his book?" I demanded.

"What book is that?" Ms. Albright asked, still speaking with caution.

"He lent me a book about epitaphs. If he's dead, then I can't give it back. I have his book and I can't give it back."

I was moving from anger to panic. I looked to Merrilee and Pascal for help. Merrilee was silently crying, wiping her eyes with the back of her sleeve. Pascal had moved to a chair and sat with his head in his hands. I couldn't see his face, but I was sure he was crying, too, the way his back was going up and down.

"I see," Ms. Albright said, studying me closely. "Would you like to bring the book in to me? I can arrange to have it returned to Mr. Creelman's family, to his wife perhaps."

"No!" This time I really did shout. "No, he trusted me with it! And besides, I'm only halfway through!"

Which was true. I was still reading Creelman's book after I woke up from my nightly nightmare, taking note of the epitaphs that could be turned into t-shirt sayings. I was even toying with the idea of making a t-shirt for Creelman, and I had been keeping an eye out for the perfect epitaph. I had pictured myself slipping the t-shirt into a blue bin along with the book, returning it to him that way, the same way he had slipped me the book in the first place.

"I'm sure you can keep it for a while," Ms. Albright said, as if speaking to a little child. She had gotten up from behind her desk and was walking over to me with her arms open.

"You don't understand," I shouted, dodging away from her in frustration. I no longer knew why I was even arguing.

I wheeled around to face Merrilee and Pascal, who refused to look my way, lost in their own sad worlds like the figures shown weeping in the library's stained-glass windows.

"This can't be happening. She doesn't know what she's talking about!" I warned them.

I stormed out of the office and back down the hallway where we had just come from. I marched into my classroom and slid behind my desk. I crossed my arms and said nothing until the lunch bell rang moments later. Then I grabbed my knapsack and headed straight for Twillingate Cemetery.

It was not a Wednesday, so I don't know what I was thinking. I just stood at the gate with all the posted warning signs and waited. Nobody came.

Not Pascal.

Not Merrilee.

Not the Brigade with their silly blue bins or clipboards or buckets.

"Derek?"

It was my mom.

And then I started crying.

I remembered snippets of Dennis's funeral — the deep organ music that thumped in my chest, the mix of heavy perfume that made it hard to breathe, the plain dark clothes that everyone wore and how the people around me were crushed together. Mr. Creelman's service was the same except that now I also wore dark clothes.

As my mom and I walked into the church, someone with silver hair and shiny shoes handed us a program with Creelman's photograph on the cover. I almost didn't recognize him because he was so much younger. And smiling.

We sat in a row toward the back. The church was nearly full. People were whispering. Candles were lit. I peered between all the heads in front of me and spotted Creelman's polished casket near the altar. It was closed, and there was a pile of white lilies on the top. Pascal walked by with his grandfather, and they sat closer to the front. He didn't see me. I didn't see Merrilee, but I knew she was there. Somewhere.

I read Creelman's program. There would be prayers and readings and hymns. Would Preeble or Wooster give the eulogy? I almost chuckled at the thought of either of them saying a few words about Creelman, let alone an entire speech in front of this large crowd. Then I felt bad for almost chuckling.

I started to read Creelman's obituary. I was surprised to learn that he had been a projectionist at a planetarium before he retired, that he had worked there for thirty-five years. His obituary went on to mention all the people in his family, a long list of names that I skimmed before turning to the back of the program. It had a picture of a wreath made of thistles.

Creelman was prickly, that's for sure. But I knew what those thistles really meant.

"The thistles are the national flower for Scotland," I whispered to my mom. "He must have had family roots in that country."

She had been watching me read the program. She gave my hand a squeeze.

"What do you think this means?" I whispered, pointing to the saying that was printed inside the wreath. It read, *All seats have an equal view of the universe.*

"I'm not sure," my mom whispered. "Perhaps it has something to do with the planetarium he worked at. Maybe it was something printed on the tickets."

I thought about him caring for the cemetery week after week. I thought about all the different cultures and religions of the people who were buried there. I thought about the elderly couple who came each year to visit their mother, and I thought about the carved stone lamb where a young child lay. I thought about Enoch's double gravestone with words only on one side, his wife buried somewhere else, perhaps somewhere far away, but still sharing the same view of the universe as Enoch.

And then I understood.

"He's saying that everyone is the same in the end," I whispered. "I bet this will be the epitaph for his gravestone."

My mom put her arm around me.

Members of Creelman's family had gathered at the back of the church and were starting to move together up the aisle to the front, where they filled the first two rows that had been saved for them. The organ changed pace, and everyone stood as the priest slowly made his way up the same aisle, followed by two others in robes. The service had begun.

There were songs. We stood to listen to the choir on the balcony with the organist. Songs about shepherds and blackbirds and souls that sing. Songs about peace. Songs about finding the way. I didn't know the words, but the man behind me had a deep singing voice and it felt good to hear him.

There were readings. I didn't really follow them. The words were old-fashioned and not the way people really talk anymore. There was something about a house with many rooms. There was something about a time to be born and a time to die. And troubled hearts. And mountains. And finishing the race.

The priest gave the eulogy. I half expected Wooster and Preeble to get up from wherever they were and stand behind the priest, handing him things on cue, just like the old days with Creelman.

I got a lump in my throat at that thought. What

would Wooster and Preeble do without Creelman?

My mom handed me some tissue.

I was glad for the tissue.

And then it was all over.

The crowd made their way out of the church, organ music trumpeting overhead, a fresh spring breeze wafting through the open oak doors. But others made their way to the front of the church and stood before Creelman's casket.

"Merrilee's up there," I said to my mom, having spotted Merrilee's red plastic jacket with the bunnies-and-carrots print. "She had cemetery duty with me and Pascal."

"So, Mr. Creelman supervised her, too?"

I nodded.

"Some people like to say goodbye before the burial," my mom whispered. "It gives them a sense of closure."

I sat, undecided.

"Do you want to say goodbye?" she asked.

I surprised myself and nodded. I guess I did want to say goodbye.

"Do you want me to come with you?" she asked.

"I'll be all right," I said.

I stood and crept up the aisle, my eyes fixed on the casket while the pews emptied around me. I slid beside Merrilee in the hushed crowd. She nodded at me, her mouth pressed into a thin line.

After a minute, she took a step forward and placed

her hand on the casket. She held it there for longer than I would have dared.

Then she took her hand away.

She turned to me.

"He's not here," she said.

She sighed.

It was a peaceful sigh.

And somehow, all the songs, all the readings and all the flowers combined did not bring me as much relief as Merrilee's three small words.

Outside, my mom and I stood on the church steps. A bagpipe player had arrived and was playing some tune I had heard before.

"'Amazing Grace,'" my mom whispered to me.

I studied the crowd.

Some were crying. Some were hugging. A few were telling stories and quietly laughing. Then the crowd parted as the casket was carried outside by the pallbearers. It was then that I spotted Preeble and Wooster, each holding up a corner and walking in formation with the others. They did not look left or right as they helped slide the casket into the long black hearse parked by the front doors of the church.

The hearse slowly drove away while members of Creelman's family got into their own cars and followed, metal doors thumping closed up and down the street.

The bagpiper played on.

"Let's go home," I said to my mom.

I had not been eating over the past few days. Suddenly, I was starving.

That night, as usual, I woke up from my nightmare, but this one was different. It started the same way.

Dennis and I were kicking the orange rubber ball. The lawnmower was buzzing in the background, the grass smelled sweet, and the sun, low on the horizon, was warm on my face.

We were laughing and laughing, and I kicked the ball extra hard. It bounced to the street. Dennis gave chase. Tires squealed. Dennis sailed through the air. Dennis lay on the pavement. The blood. Me, frozen on the sidewalk. A crowd forming around Dennis.

Then someone put a comforting hand on my shoulder. I turned to look. It was Creelman. He was not scowling. Instead, he tried to speak, but he could only mouth his silent words over and over while sadly shaking his head. It was like watching a movie without the audio.

"What are you saying?" I asked, straining to hear. "I don't understand."

He mouthed his words over and over, but I couldn't hear a thing.

"What?" I shouted, and my own shouting woke me up.

The door to my bedroom opened.

"Derek," my mom said. "You're having a nightmare." She came into the room and sat on my bed. "I'll turn on your lamp."

I shifted to a sitting position, my pajamas soaked in sweat as my eyes adjusted to the light.

"It was about Dennis," I said. "Mr. Creelman was in it, too."

"You've had a bad shock," my mom said. "This was bound to happen."

"I've been having nightmares for a while," I admitted.

"How long?" she asked.

"Months."

"Why didn't you tell me?"

"You get too worried. And besides, the last time I complained, we ended up moving to another town."

"Derek, we didn't move just because of the accident. I was offered another job, remember?"

"No," I corrected her. "I remember overhearing you and Dad talking about me needing a fresh start."

My mom was silent.

"Fair enough," she allowed. "But you were a troubled little boy. You're older now, so tell me what you need."

I thought for a minute. What had Creelman been trying to say to me? If I could figure that out, maybe it would put an end to my nightmares once and for all. At least, that was what I hoped.

THE SPOTTED DOG LAST SEEN | 135

"I think I should stay home tomorrow," I said, slipping back under the covers. "Just for one day. I'm really tired."

"Of course," my mom said.

We both knew the real reason. Tomorrow was Wednesday, but cemetery duty had been cancelled, and the school had not yet figured out what to do with the three of us for the remaining few weeks in the year.

She tucked me in and turned out the light.

When she got to the door, she paused and said, "Promise me one thing."

"What?" I asked in the dark.

"Promise you'll tell me if things get worse."

"I promise," I said.

She quietly shut the door.

That morning, the telephone rang. My mom, who had decided to work from home for the day, answered it.

"Derek! Telephone!" she called.

I picked up the phone.

"Hello?"

"Why weren't you in school?" Merrilee demanded. "Are you sick?"

"No, just really tired," I said.

"Are you coming in tomorrow?" she asked.

"Why?"

"Because Pascal and I have compared notes, and we worked out that the best time of the week to open

Trevor Tower's locker is tomorrow afternoon. A musician is coming to visit the school, so a bunch of grades will be practicing with her in the music room across from his locker and the class door will be closed. Ideal conditions!"

The time capsule. That was the last thing on my mind.

"Are you still there?" she asked.

"Yes," I said.

"Will you be in tomorrow? The school year is almost over. We're running out of time."

"Yes," I said, and I hung up.

"Who was that?" my mom asked from where she lingered in the kitchen, pretending to wipe the counter.

"Merrilee."

"The girl in the church?"

"Yes."

"Was she worried about you?" my mom asked.

"I guess," I said with a shrug.

It seemed easier to give her that answer than to explain how Merrilee and Pascal were desperate to open a mysterious locker assigned to someone entirely unknown to us, having broken a secret code that had been written in a series of public library mystery books.

"That's nice," my mom said. "Would you like something to eat?"

"Sure," I said.

At least my appetite was back.

After lunch, I spent the afternoon working on a new t-shirt based on a story I had heard on the radio while I was eating. A politician took four live beavers to China in the hope that he could trade them for a rare panda bear to take home to a zoo. He failed. They gave him a common elk instead. My t-shirt featured four beavers, a not-equal sign and one panda.

I was pleased with the design and planned to wear it to school the next day instead of my regular school uniform. I remembered that Queensview was holding a fundraiser, and students could wear their street clothes for the day if they gave a small donation.

Still, I had an uneasy time falling asleep that night, tossing and turning over what secrets we might discover in Trevor Tower's locker. But when my alarm clock went off in the morning, I was grateful that at least I had not had the nightmare.

Pascal scrambled up the front steps of the school to join me as I entered the building for my first class.

"Merrilee says to meet her at Trevor Tower's locker at 2:25 p.m."

"But we're in math class at 2:25 p.m."

"That's right. I'll make an excuse to go to the bathroom. Then a few minutes later, you'll make an excuse, too. We'll rendezvous at the locker."

"Rendezvous? Good grief! What kind of word is that?"

"Rendezvous. It's a spy word. Get with the program!"

He scooted off down the hall.

The morning went by as usual, but I decided to pay Ms. Albright a visit when lunchtime arrived. She was at her desk.

"Oh, hello, Derek. I'm so glad to see you back at school."

"Thanks," I said.

I was not sure how to begin.

"Your t-shirt," Ms. Albright said. "Is that about the story they told on the radio yesterday?"

I nodded.

"I heard that story, too! I can't imagine why anyone would want to trade a magnificent panda for four ordinary beavers. You've done a marvelous job!"

"Thanks," I said, aware that if I didn't stop with my one-word answers, I was going to sound like a complete idiot.

"Ms. Albright," I plowed ahead, "I'm sorry for how I acted the other day and whatnot."

"Don't you worry about that," she said with a wave of her hand. "It was quite a shock, I'm sure. How was the funeral service?"

"The church was packed," I said.

"Mr. Creelman was very special, very rare indeed."

"Kind of like a panda," I said, looking down at my t-shirt.

"Exactly," Ms. Albright replied. "Maybe you had

Mr. Creelman in the back of your mind when you made it."

She had that right. Mr. Creelman was in the back of my mind, trapped in my nightmares along with Dennis.

"I'm sure I did," I said. "Well, I should get back."

"Glad you dropped by," Ms. Albright said.

All too soon, it was math class.

At 2:18 p.m., Pascal put up his hand to leave. He shot me a sly smile as he went out the door. My heart started to pound.

2:19.

2:20.

2:21.

2:21 and thirty seconds.

I held up my shaky hand.

"Yes, Derek?"

"May I be excused?"

"Be quick. We're about to review fractions."

I fumbled for the door and stood in the hall. It was empty. I took a deep breath, then crept up the stairwell to the second floor. I spotted Pascal at the far end, practically bouncing from one foot to the other in front of Trevor's locker.

"Where's Merrilee?" I whispered.

"Don't know," Pascal replied. "But we can't wait forever. We've got to get back to math class."

We stood with uncertainty, startling at every little noise.

And then after what seemed like forever, the door to a classroom far down the hall opened. It was Merrilee. She slipped out of the room and closed the door behind her without a peep.

"Let's do it," she whispered as soon as she was within earshot.

The three of us stood staring at the locker.

"Who's going to open it?" I asked.

Nobody budged.

"Go for it," I whispered to no one in particular.

More silence.

"Pascal!" Merrilee whispered.

"Why me?" he asked, spinning to face her.

"I'm busy on the lookout," she whispered. "And Derek's wearing a confusing t-shirt that makes me think he's not up for the challenge."

"Ms. Albright understood my t-shirt," I countered.

Still, nobody moved.

"We're running out of time," Merrilee warned.

"Oh, for crying out loud," Pascal said.

He took a bold step forward and grabbed the lock.

"What's the combination again?"

"Twenty-eight. Thirty-four. Eighteen," I announced, proving to Merrilee that I was not confused.

"Hey, that's quite good for someone who wears pandas and beavers, something I wouldn't be caught dead in."

This from a girl who wore a red plastic jacket with bunnies and carrots on it.

"One panda. Four beavers," I snapped. "There's a difference."

Merrilee and I were cut short by the sound of a click that echoed down the empty hallway.

Pascal had opened the lock.

Nine

Obituary

PASCAL SLID the lock off the hasp.

"Here we go," he whispered hoarsely.

He slowly opened the door, which gave an alarming creak, then took a giant step back to join Merrilee and me. The three of us stared at the contents.

The first thing that struck me was how ordinary everything looked. Nothing jumped out at us or vaporized or smelled rotten. Instead, there was a single slim book on the top shelf. Below the shelf was a heap of envelopes on the floor of the locker. The envelopes were in different colors, assorted sizes and various thicknesses.

Merrilee reached in and grabbed the book from the top shelf. It had a picture on the cover of a dog with spots that was curled up and half hidden under a park bench in a cemetery.

"*The Spotted Dog Last Seen*," she said, reading the cover, "'by Murray Easton.'"

The Spotted Dog Last Seen? I had heard that title before. But where?

She flipped through the pages, pausing whenever she got to chapter headings.

"Who is Murray Easton?" Pascal demanded. "I thought this was Trevor Tower's locker."

Merrilee flipped to the end of the book and landed on the back page.

"'About the author,'" she read out loud.

We gathered in.

"'Murray Easton loves yard sales and is often inspired by odd objects that are no longer wanted. His collection of poems, *Treadmill, Hardly Used*, won the national Writers of Tomorrow Award and received starred reviews in numerous literary journals. He lives with his wife and an excitable dog in a small town called Ferndale. They both have an ear for good dialogue. This is Murray's first novel.'"

"I used to live in Ferndale," I said in awe.

We looked at each other, thinking over Murray Easton's biography. Merrilee flipped to the front of the book. She paused on the dedication page, then tightened her grip on the cover. I thought it was because she had discovered another secret code penciled in the margin, but I was wrong.

Dead wrong.

"*To the Queensview Mystery Book Club*," she read out loud.

Then below that, written by hand, were the words *Tell the Club that Buster's doing fine*. It was followed by Murray Easton's signature.

"I didn't know that Queensview has a Mystery Book Club," I said.

"It doesn't," Merrilee said. "At least, not anymore. And look at the publication date. This book was printed *after* the time capsule was locked."

Pascal made the next move. He grabbed a handful of envelopes from the pile below and flipped through them while Merrilee and I peered over his shoulders. The envelopes were all addressed to the same person — Mr. Easton. Each one was written in different handwriting. Pascal turned the first few over.

"They're sealed," he observed.

He put all but the top one back and went to slip his finger beneath the flap of the envelope he still held so that he could tear it open.

"Stop!" I warned, rescuing the envelope from Pascal. "Envelopes are like coffins. They're sealed for a reason!"

"The plot thickens," Merrilee said, as if she had just tasted something delicious. "And I can tell you this. Murray Easton is not the one behind the secret codes that led us to this locker."

"How do you know?" I asked, still trying to piece together where I had heard the title of Murray Easton's book before.

"Penmanship," she stated matter-of-factly.

"Penmanship?" Pascal repeated.

"That's right," Merrilee said. "Think back to the codes. How would you describe that writing?"

"Tidy," I said. "But cramped. And the letter *a* was written with a hood on it."

"Now look at the handwriting on the dedication page."

Pascal and I studied the writing. It was loopy and slanted backwards, like left-handers do. Not the same at all. Besides, the letter *a* in the word *that* did not have a hood.

"Okay, time's up," Merrilee said. "Let's put everything back the way we found it for now."

We quickly returned the materials, and Pascal slid the lock back on the hasp with a click. He spun the dial, then turned to face us.

"Now what?" he asked.

"Everyone needs to return to class as if nothing has happened," Merrilee instructed.

"Nothing *has* happened!" I said, feeling let down and frustrated in equal measure.

But Merrilee did not stick around to argue. She strode all the way down the hall, opened the door to her class and silently slipped inside.

"*The Spotted Dog Last Seen*," I said. "Where have I read that before?"

Pascal shrugged. It was his turn to start down the hallway, his shoes squeaking on the tile floor.

"Give me a couple of minutes before you head back," he called over his shoulder. "It will be less suspicious if we don't arrive together."

I stood awkwardly in front of Trevor Tower's locker.

"*The Spotted Dog Last Seen*," I whispered at it, having been abandoned in the hallway. "Last seen where?"

The answer, of course, was inside that locker. I might as well have been standing in front of Enoch Pettypiece's grave marker at Twillingate Cemetery. I could ask as many questions as I wanted, but I would only get blank silence in return. I would have to dig deeper.

It was then that I did something rash. Maybe it was because of the lack of sleep all those nights and whatnot.

Twenty-eight. Thirty-four. Eighteen.

Click.

I reopened the locker.

I left the sealed envelopes alone, but I figured that books were meant to be read. I grabbed the one on the top shelf, then shut the door and secured the lock with clumsy hands as quietly as I could in my haste.

I had trouble breathing as I scrambled down the stairs to my own locker. I shoved the book deep inside my knapsack, then dashed the door shut. By the time I returned to class, my hands were sweating and my chest was pounding. I refused to make eye contact with Pascal as I slid behind my desk.

That night, Creelman returned to my nightmare, mouthing silent words on my front lawn after the accident and sadly shaking his head.

"I can't hear you!" I gasped as I bolted upright in my bed.

I turned my lamp on. Two books now lay on my night table — Creelman's *Famous Last Words* and Murray Easton's *The Spotted Dog Last Seen*.

I had almost finished reading Creelman's collection of epitaphs, so I picked up that book and started flipping through. Then, on a hunch, I turned to the chapter on epitaphs for pets, which I had already read.

And there it was. Third epitaph down. Epitaph for a beloved fire-station mascot, lost in the line of duty.

> *The spotted dog last seen*
> *patrolling ladders touching skies*
> *now rests beneath the green*
> *and our tapestry of sighs.*

I put the epitaph book aside. I knew I'd seen Murray Easton's title before! Did Creelman know Murray Easton? Had Creelman lent him this very book? I picked up *The Spotted Dog Last Seen* and started to read.

"The school secretary called," my mom reported to me as soon as I got home that Friday afternoon.

I had been a bit edgy all day, thinking that Merrilee or Pascal might discover I had taken Murray Easton's book without them knowing. But I was certain the call from the secretary had nothing to do with that.

"Apparently, Mr. Creelman made a large donation of books to the public library, and somebody named Loyola Louden called the school to say that they could use your help in cataloguing the books. So, the thought is that you could report to the library next Wednesday to complete your community service before school is let out for the summer. Does that sound okay to you?"

She was still treating me as if I was going to break down at any minute.

"Sure," I said. "What's for dinner?"

My nightly dreams continued over the weekend, except now I could count on the fact that Creelman would show up at the scene of the accident mouthing his silent words with that woeful look. Then I would wake up and flip through the pages of Murray Easton's book to where I had left off.

The Spotted Dog Last Seen was good. It was about a language arts teacher who taught a lot of his classes by doing unusual projects. One week, he had his students write poems about the sky on kites that they built. Then they flew the kites in the schoolyard. Another week, he brought in boxes of dated textbooks and had his students make birdhouses out of them to hang from the playground equipment. During another week still, he took a manuscript he had been working on and had his students fold the pages into bats or dragonflies, turning them into mobiles of fluttering words marked up by red ink.

By the time the weekend was almost over, I had gotten to the part where the teacher wrote about a small dog that his students had started to feed every lunchtime. He asked them about it, about the spotted dog he had last seen by the school's fence. They told him that the dog was a stray, and when it ended up at the animal shelter, the teacher adopted it.

The dog proved to be quite a handful. It would tear around the teacher's house in excitement each day when he returned home. The only way that he could calm the dog down was to read a story out loud. He soon discovered that the dog liked movie scripts the best, curling up with its head on its spotted paws to listen.

I reread Murray Easton's biography at the end. He had an excitable dog who also had a good ear for dialogue. Was Murray Easton writing about himself? Was Murray Easton a teacher? I reread the dedication page. *To the Queensview Mystery Book Club.* Had he been Trevor Tower's teacher at Queensview? Then I reread the handwritten note below. *Tell the Club that Buster's doing fine!* Was Buster the spotted stray dog?

I returned to the story. I must have read the book halfway into the night, even though I knew I had school in the morning. Eventually, I fell asleep, along with the excitable spotted dog.

It was Monday morning. I was climbing the front steps of the school when Pascal rushed them two at a time to join me as I opened the door.

"I was walking past the cemetery on the way here when a truck came by," he reported. "They were delivering Creelman's grave marker. It's supposed to be installed this morning."

"So soon?" I said.

Pascal nodded as we made our way to the side of the hallway to continue our conversation in private, while noisy crowds of students shuffled past us on their way to their classes.

"Creelman must have designed his grave marker in advance, just like our homework assignment," Pascal said. "Want to go check it out at lunch? Pay our respects and all?"

Creelman. He had been visiting me so often in my dreams that I still had a hard time thinking of him as gone.

"Well, do you?" Pascal asked. "We could grab Merrilee and review our case while we're there. He'll be located in the newer section with the granites."

It was one thing to return to the cemetery and pore over the gravestone of someone I had never met. Take

Enoch, for example. His half-blank marker did not haunt me one bit. But it would be another thing to visit Creelman. I know Creelman. Correction. I knew Creelman. And I could still picture his scowl and remember his lessons, every one of them.

Still. Creelman was haunting my dreams. Would visiting his gravesite make his silent words come to life so that I could hear them?

"Okay," I said with resolve. "But only if it's not raining. Otherwise, I'll meet you in the library with Colonel Mustard and the lead pipe."

Pascal peered with a puzzled look through the window beside the front door at the perfectly clear blue sky. He didn't get my little joke about the murder mystery board game *Clue*.

Merrilee met us at the iron gate at noon, still sporting her red plastic bunnies-and-carrots jacket.

"Just like old times," she said when we arrived.

Pascal led us inside. We made our way past all the old slates and sandstones toppling this way and that, past the marbles with their sugared statues and the less-common obelisks with their pretentious heights and headed for the modern granites beyond the first hedge-row in the north section. The birds were singing, but otherwise we had the whole cemetery to ourselves.

"I'm still confused," Pascal admitted while we walked. "What does Murray Easton have to do with

Trevor Tower? What's with all those letters in the locker written to Mr. Easton? And who's been writing secret codes in mystery books at the public library that led us to the locker in the first place? I just don't get any of it."

"We'll figure things out," Merrilee said, more marching than walking. "We don't know much about Trevor Tower, but we do know that Murray Easton is a writer and that *The Spotted Dog Last Seen* is his first novel. He hasn't written anything since, at least not yet."

We stared at her.

"I looked up his name at the public library," she explained, "to borrow *The Spotted Dog Last Seen*. The library has several copies, but they were all signed out."

A wave of guilt slowed my pace. She still didn't know about the signed copy on my night table.

"How can we find out more about Trevor Tower?" I asked, trying to distract them.

What I really wanted to do was buy time to finish the book I had swiped from the locker. I was convinced that it was the key to everything.

"We can't ask Loyola any more questions. She'd just get suspicious," Merrilee warned. "But I know a great place where we can find out more about Trevor."

"Where?" Pascal and I asked together.

"The public library. It has a whole shelf of Queensview yearbooks in the archives section upstairs where the church choir used to sing. I've seen it."

"We're going there on Wednesday to catalogue

Creelman's books," Pascal said. "Let's look up Trevor Tower then."

Pascal stopped short.

"Here it is," he said, pointing to a freshly dug plot.

We turned to face Creelman's gravestone.

I paused, expecting to keel over like I had done when I had come across the carved stone lamb, but I didn't. I took slow steadying breaths while reading Creelman's gravestone. It featured thistles and, sure enough, there was the epitaph I had read in his program — *All seats have an equal view of the universe.*

"He was a projectionist at a planetarium," Merrilee explained.

"I know," I said. "I read his obituary at the funeral."

"I'm sad for his wife and daughter," Pascal said.

"He had a daughter?" I asked.

"You said you read the obituary," Merrilee said.

"Not the whole thing," I admitted. "Just the part about him being a projectionist."

"I met them at the church," Pascal said.

"Who? His wife and daughter?" I asked.

"Yes. I told them about our work at Twillingate Cemetery with the Brigade. They knew all about the Brigade, about Wooster and Preeble. Then they told me how they decided that Twillingate Cemetery was the best place to bury Creelman."

"Why wouldn't it be? He loves this place. *Loved* this place," I corrected myself.

"Yes, they came to realize that. But his grandson — his daughter's boy — is buried at another cemetery. So at first they wondered whether Creelman should have been buried in the same place. They told me that he had been very close to his grandson."

"Wait. Did you say *grandson*?" I asked.

"Yes. Why?"

I didn't answer right away. Instead, I thought back to my lunch with Creelman. I tried to remember what he had told me about cemeteries, that there were no ghosts, no vampires and no zombies, but that people could still be haunted. He had said that they could be troubled by past events, by things not resolved.

My heart started to pound.

"How old was Creelman's grandson when he died?" I asked Pascal.

Pascal shrugged. "I didn't ask that."

"Where is his grandson buried?" I asked.

"I didn't ask that, either."

"Come on, Pascal. Think!"

"I don't know. Some nearby town, I guess. Ferndale? That's it. His daughter had to drive in for Creelman's service. That's all I know."

I turned to Merrilee.

"Do you remember the grandson's name?" I demanded, panic rising in my throat.

"No. I didn't memorize the obituary. What's going on?"

I couldn't answer. The swirling pieces of my recurring nightmare were starting to connect in ways that would change everything.

I tore out of the cemetery as fast as I could and headed straight to the church, four blocks away, where Creelman's funeral had been held.

"Wait!" Pascal shouted. "Where are you going?"

I didn't slow down.

"Derek!" Merrilee joined in.

"Wait!" Pascal repeated.

I didn't stop until I reached the church. I flew up the granite steps and yanked on the enormous oak doors.

Locked.

I collapsed on the steps, out of breath.

Merrilee and Pascal caught up. Merrilee sat beside me, while Pascal stood blocking my escape.

"What's happening?" Merrilee asked.

"I need to get a copy of Creelman's program," I said.

"Why?"

"I need to read it. I need to read the whole thing. I need to read the part about his grandson."

"Hang on," Merrilee said. She reached into her jacket pocket. "I think I still might have a copy."

She fished out a harmonica and a folded piece of paper. She unfolded it. It was Creelman's program with the thistle wreath and the photograph of him when he was younger.

"Here," she said, handing it to me.

I pushed the program back to her.

"No. You read it, " I insisted, still out of breath. "Tell me the name of Creelman's grandson, the one who died."

Merrilee opened the program and read the obituary to herself. When she finished, she refolded the program and stuffed it back in her pocket along with the harmonica.

"Dennis," she said. "His grandson's name was Dennis."

Ten

Yearbook

MERRILEE WAS NOT a vampire or a werewolf or some other form of the undead, and there were no ghosts in the cemetery. I was certain of all that. So when I learned that Creelman's grandson was Dennis — *my friend Dennis* — I didn't for a second think that Creelman was haunting me. I knew his visits were all in my head.

The facts were the facts, and I explained them to Merrilee and Pascal as plainly as I could.

"I once had a friend named Dennis," I said. "He was hit by a car when we were little."

"And you think your friend was Creelman's grandson?" Merrilee asked.

"Yes."

"How can you be sure?"

"I'm from Ferndale. So was Dennis. That's where he was buried."

Merrilee fell silent.

Pascal sat down beside me.

"Did Creelman know you knew Dennis?" he asked.

"I think so," I said. "I told him about my nightmare."

"What nightmare?"

"I have this recurring nightmare about Dennis. About the accident."

"What did Creelman say when you told him?"

I thought back to our lunch with the meat loaves. I thought about how he stared out the window, distant, after I told him about Dennis. Even the waitress could not get his attention when she came by with a second cup of coffee.

It all made sense now.

"He didn't say much," I reported. "But he did tell me that people can be troubled by past events. They can be haunted because of things not resolved."

"Was he talking about you, or was he talking about himself?"

"Me, I thought. But now I don't know."

I stopped short of reporting that Creelman was now visiting me in my nightmares, desperately trying to tell me something. Perhaps Creelman had been talking about himself back at the cafe.

Or perhaps I was slowly going crazy because of lack of sleep. I had already sneaked Murray Easton's novel out of the time capsule. Who knew what I was capable of doing next?

It was a scary thought.

"What a strange coincidence," I said, probably a bit too jovially for the situation. I stood to let them know that the discussion was over.

"Yes," Pascal said, looking at Merrilee with doubt. "It is."

"I'm sorry about your friend Dennis," Merrilee added haltingly. "And I'm sorry that Creelman lost his grandson."

"Thanks," I said, and left it at that.

"So, are we all on for Wednesday at the library?" Merrilee asked, getting up from the steps. "Loyola showed me the boxes of books that Creelman donated."

"I'll be there," I said.

"Me, too," Pascal said. "But you know what? And I never thought I'd say this. It won't be nearly as interesting as cemetery duty."

He was right.

When I arrived at the public library on Wednesday, Pascal and Merrilee were already there. They were sitting at the large oak tables in the research area, past all the stacks, just like before. I half expected the Brigade to appear, and I let that thought linger before I told myself I was being foolish.

"Hi, everyone," Loyola said, almost as soon as I sat down.

She had appeared from a row of stacks and was

wheeling a squeaky trolley of books to be re-shelved.

"Thanks so much for helping out. As you can see, Creelman had a large collection."

I twisted in my chair to see at least twenty cardboard boxes stacked neatly to the side.

"Good grief!" I said.

Loyola continued. "Apparently, he was in the process of packing up his books to donate to the library, because he and his wife were getting ready to sell their house. They wanted to downsize into something they could manage more easily."

"Downsize?" repeated Pascal.

"Move to a smaller house," Loyola explained. "What I'd like you to do is go through the boxes and sort the books into three piles according to our collections policy."

Loyola pulled out a file from her trolley and removed several sheets of paper.

"This table will be for approvals," she said, laying a sheet of paper with *Approvals* written in black felt marker on one table. "This table will be for sales." She laid a sheet with *Sales* written down on the next table. "This table will be for recycling." She laid a final sheet of paper with the word *Recycling* on the third table.

I glanced up at the stained-glass windows that surrounded us. The sun beamed down in spectacular colors. I could see why the Brigade took the time to restore them.

"The first thing you need to understand is that accepting books is very costly."

"Costly? Creelman donated these books. Donate means free, right?" Pascal asked.

"The books may be free, but it costs a lot of staff time to process and catalogue the books, and then provide the shelf space to house them. So, we're very picky when it comes to what we will actually accept."

I must have looked alarmed, because Loyola quickly added, "We make sure that we tell all our donors. Creelman knew this, too."

"How do you decide?" Merrilee asked.

Loyola went to one of the boxes, opened it and took out a book. She held it up.

"Easy. Here's what you need to ask. Is the book in excellent condition?" She looked at the book's cover and flipped through the pages. She even smelled it. "If the answer is no, then you send the book right to recycling. The library does not accept books that are yellowed, water damaged or moldy."

"Who donates moldy books?" Pascal asked.

"You'd be surprised," Loyola said. "We also get a lot of books that smell like cigarette smoke. Those get recycled, too."

"Creelman smoked," I said quietly.

"He did," Loyola replied. "But his wife told us that he never smoked inside his house where the books were kept."

"Plus he was trying to quit," I added, feeling as if I should defend Creelman in some small way.

Both Merrilee and Pascal nodded in agreement, while Loyola handed lengthy stapled-together lists to each of us that she took from the file on her trolley.

"Say the book is in excellent condition," Loyola continued, "like this one. You then need to ask if the book fills a gap in the library's collection. Generally, there are two types of gaps — new bestsellers and books with subjects that are currently popular. Time travel. Vampires. The *Titanic*. These are a few examples from the list of popular book subjects I've just handed you. We're interested in these books because they have longer wait lists and there is a high demand for them. That means there's a gap."

She turned to the cover of the book again and read it out loud. "*Projector Troubleshooting and Repair: A Diagnostic Guide for the Apollo Viewlux, the Nova III and the Observa-Dome.*"

She looked at us.

"I think we can all agree that this one is neither a bestseller nor a book of popular interest."

Without another word, Loyola slid the condemned book onto the sales table.

"What happens to books on the sales table?" I asked.

"We have a volunteer group who organize a book sale each year. The profits go back to the library to help buy new books and equipment that we really

need. Creelman's donation will help make a big difference."

"So, ending up on the sales table is better than being recycled," I muttered, glancing at sad Table Number
Three.

"Any questions?" Loyola asked.

"What if we come across rare books?" Merrilee
asked. "Shouldn't you make a table for those?"

Pascal weighed in. "Rare? As in undercooked?"

"I think Merrilee means *rare* as in *uncommon*,"
Loyola said. "A rare book would be an old first edition.
Or maybe a book signed by a deceased author. Or maybe a book privately printed by someone famous. Or
even a beautiful book with a leather cover, printed on
exotic paper or containing hand-drawn illustrations."

She turned to Merrilee.

"Don't worry. I'll review the piles you sort before
anything further is done to the books." Loyola turned
to me. "Nice t-shirt."

I looked down at my shirt. It read, *Careful, or you'll
star in my next novel.* I specifically chose it that morning because of library duty. I was glad she noticed.

With that, Loyola pushed her squeaky trolley back
up the main aisle, past all the stacks to the front desk,
and we were left facing twenty or so bulging boxes.

"I was right. Cemetery duty was way better," Pascal
said glumly.

"It's just for today," I said. "And then we're done."

"That's right," Pascal said, instantly cheering up. "I thought that our three-month assignment for community service was going to last forever. But now we have less than a week left before summer holidays!"

"Time flies," I said, thinking back to the gravestones at Twillingate that featured an hourglass tipped on its side with wings.

We each grabbed a box and started to sort the books. Books about cemetery art. Books about poetry. Books about astronomy and starry heavens. Books about lunar missions. Books about how to make a telescope. Books of science fiction.

We checked the poetry books for author signatures. We checked the astronomy books for beautiful illustrations. We checked the science fiction for first editions.

In the end, most of them went straight to sales, except for two. Merrilee placed a book about our solar system on the recycling table because it still referred to Pluto as a planet. Pascal placed a book about rockets on the recycling table because the cover was marked up with crayons, and some of the pictures had been cut out with crooked scissor strokes.

That book made me think of Dennis with his grandfather. I slammed my mind's garage door shut by keeping busy.

"Want to take a break?" Merrilee asked, about an hour into our task.

She nodded slyly toward the balcony, the archives.

I remembered the yearbooks. Pascal and I nodded eagerly.

We followed her upstairs, where the church choir used to sit. She led us to one of the stacks, then bent down on her knees.

"Here's the collection from Queensview," she advised.

"Okay. We're looking for the one that was published seven years ago," I said, joining her on my knees, "when Trevor Tower was a student in grade six, and he was selected for the time-capsule program."

She ran her fingers over the spines, mouthing the years to herself. She stopped and pulled one out.

"This is it."

We stood. Pascal and I peered over her shoulder as she opened the yearbook and turned the pages, pausing as she hit the classroom photographs. She read the grades and teachers' names out loud.

"Grade one: Ms. Henderson. Grade two: Mr. Nickelson. Grade three: Mr. Battersby. Grade four: Ms. Chow. Hey, that's Ms. Chow. I had her in grade four."

"We all did," I said. "Keep going."

"Grade five: Ms. Matthews. Had her, too, last year. She looks old even back then!"

"She gave me an A on my science fair project," Pascal said. "It was the first one I ever got."

"Really?" I said. "Is this what we want to do? Talk about our marks and whatnot? Give me that."

I grabbed the yearbook from Merrilee to get on with it. I turned the page.

"Grade six: Mr. Easton."

Merrilee and Pascal gasped. No one noticed that I wasn't surprised.

We leaned in for a better look.

Like all the other teachers, Mr. Easton stood to the left of his class. He was wearing a suit jacket and runners. He had thick wavy hair. He was smiling, the kind of smile that happens after a really big laugh. And he reminded me of the main character in *The Spotted Dog Last Seen*.

"He looks sad," Merrilee remarked.

"What are you talking about?" I asked.

"I can see it in his eyes," she said quietly.

Merrilee scanned the list of students' names below the photograph. We already knew who two of them would be.

"Look. Loyola Louden."

We peered at a much younger Loyola who was grinning from ear to ear in the middle of the back row. She was super tall, even back then.

"And look. Trevor Tower."

She pointed to a skinny boy with his arms crossed, looking away from the camera from where he sat at the far end of the front row.

"Does Mr. Easton show up anywhere else?" Pascal asked, taking the yearbook from me.

"Try the school club section," I suggested, thinking back to who Murray Easton had dedicated his book to — the Queensview Mystery Book Club.

Pascal flipped through those pages. Chess Club. Science Club. Debating Club. Mystery Book Club.

"Stop," Merrilee said. "Stop."

"There he is again," Pascal said in awe.

Mr. Easton was pictured with a group of students sitting in a circle outside on the soccer field. Only there wasn't a soccer ball in sight. Instead, they were all busy reading. My guess was that they were reading mystery books, just like in his novel.

"This still doesn't explain how Murray Easton's book got into Trevor's locker," Merrilee said. "His book was published after the time capsule was sealed, so he couldn't have added it while he was teaching at Queensview. Besides, by the time his book was published, he had moved to Ferndale. Remember the biography in his book?"

"You're right," I said. "And Loyola told us that Trevor Tower also moved away right after grade six."

"Ms. Albright told us that, too," Merrilee said. "So we know that neither Murray Easton nor Trevor Tower could have put the book inside."

Merrilee paused in thought. Then she continued.

"Mr. Easton obviously loved mystery books, but we also know that he wasn't behind writing the secret codes because we compared penmanship. The handwriting we found in his own novel and the penciled lists in the margins of the other mystery books in the library do not match."

"So who then? Who's been writing the codes? And who put Murray Easton's book into Trevor's locker?" Pascal asked.

Merrilee grabbed the yearbook back from Pascal and began to read the names of the students in the mystery book club out loud.

"'Pictured clockwise are Noah Tupper, Trevor Tower, Jennifer Bates...'" Merrilee paused and gulped. "'Loyola Louden.'"

"Loyola Louden!" Pascal repeated, a bit too loudly.

"Shhhhh!" she said.

Without another word, the three of us crept over to the edge of the balcony and had a look below. Loyola was seated at the front desk helping some teenagers sign out books. We pulled back before she looked up.

Merrilee shut the yearbook and returned it to the shelf. When she stood, she looked at the two of us with a frown.

"There can only be one person who's been writing secret codes in the mystery books at this library. And I am betting it's the same person who put Murray Easton's novel into Trevor Tower's locker."

I was sure I knew the answer.

Loyola Louden.

But neither Pascal nor I ventured a guess out loud. In fact, no one made a move.

"How can ..." I managed to squeeze some words out, "... how can we be sure?"

"Once again, penmanship," Merrilee said matter-of-factly.

"Penmanship?" I repeated.

"Remember how we described the writing of the secret codes in the mystery novels?" she asked.

I jumped in to answer.

"Tidy. Cramped. Makes the letter *a* with a hood on top."

"We need to compare that description to Loyola's writing," Merrilee said.

"Where are we going to get a sample of Loyola's writing?" I asked.

"We already have it," Merrilee said, studying me to see if I could connect the dots.

"She's right," I said to Pascal. "We have the labels on the tables downstairs that we've been sorting Creelman's books by."

It was all we could do not to bolt down the stairs to the research area and snatch a label to study. Instead, we formed a line, single file, and with great restraint stiffly returned to the main floor where we had been sorting books, eyes darting in every direction. We halted in front of the sales table with one book on it. My t-shirt was sticking to my back.

The word *Sales* was written tidily but the letters were jammed together in the center of the paper, with all kinds of white space around them. Sure enough, the letter *a* had a hood on it. Pascal silently pointed out the dead giveaway with his finger.

My mouth went dry and my next words were hoarse. "What now?"

"We confront her," Merrilee said with deadly aim. "We find out what's behind all this."

"What? *Now?*" I asked, both hoarse and alarmed.

I looked at Pascal and even his eyes were wide, wide open.

"Yes, now," Merrilee said as she pushed her glasses up higher on her nose.

Merrilee didn't wait for us. She spun on her heels and strode down the main aisle toward the front desk where Loyola sat rearranging her bulletin board.

Pascal and I turned to each other.

"Do we wait here, or what?" he asked.

We peered past the stacks to see that Merrilee had almost made her entire way to the front desk. She did not look back or slow her stride.

"No, we'd better join her," I said, without much bravery.

"I'll follow you," Pascal said, taking a step behind me.

I made my way down the aisle, straining to hear sounds of an interrogation. I was surprised to reach the front desk without hearing anything of the sort.

At least, not yet.

Instead, Merrilee seemed to be having a pleasant chat with Loyola about not much.

"Loyola was just rearranging her lost-and-found bulletin board," Merrilee explained in a friendly tone as soon as we arrived. But as she spoke, she kept her eyes trained on Loyola. She was plotting something. I was dead certain of that.

"I see you've kept your favorite teacher's comment up."

I followed her lead and looked at Loyola's bulletin board. There, still folded and pinned, was the front cover of Loyola's essay about how she had *not* spent her summer vacation.

"What did your teacher write on the cover?" Merrilee asked sweetly.

She leaned across the desk to unpin the paper. She turned it around to face her, flattened out the folds and cleared her throat.

"*Loyola, you are a gifted storyteller. Promise me that you'll keep writing.*"

She looked up at Loyola. "Speaking of writing," Merrilee continued with alarming cheeriness, "we recently came across an interesting book."

"You did?" Loyola asked, easing into the trap.

She looked past Merrilee to me and Pascal. We just stood like wordless lumps.

Like Wooster and Preeble.

"And you wouldn't believe where we found it," Merrilee said like silk.

"Where?" Loyola asked.

"A locker," Merrilee said.

"That's not unusual, is it?" Loyola said. "Isn't that the kind of thing you would find in a locker? School supplies, books, gym clothes ... "

Her voice drifted off because she began to busy herself by processing a pile of returned books.

"Not just any locker," Merrilee continued. Her voice was no longer as friendly. It had hardened on the edges. She started to pound on every word, like Creelman had done with his fist on the table. "Trevor Tower's locker."

"Trevor Tower? My old grade-six classmate?" Loyola asked, still processing returned books.

"None other," Merrilee said.

"What were you doing in Trevor's locker? That's a time capsule. You're not supposed to open it for fifty years," she said, not looking Merrilee in the eye.

"You know why!"

Merrilee's bold accusation felt like a deadly blow. It swept across the entire first floor of the library, smashing against each and every stack all the way to the back where we had been sorting Creelman's books. When I looked around, I half expected to see the stacks toppling this away and that, just like the gravestones back at the cemetery.

"What do you mean?" Loyola asked casually, but she stopped processing books.

Merrilee leaned toward Loyola, their faces barely apart.

"It was *you*. *You* wrote the secret codes in the mystery novels."

"Secret codes?" Loyola repeated, but even I could see that she was pretending. She was just too calm.

"Don't deny it," Merrilee demanded.

Loyola opened her mouth as if to say something, but then paused. She studied Merrilee, then Pascal, then me.

"What gave me away?" she asked us, smiling as she said it.

Eleven

Mystery Book Club

LOYOLA'S SMILE did not unnerve Merrilee one bit as she extracted her confession. I had never seen her so dead serious. Not in the cemetery. Not at the church. Not even while breaking into the locker.

"Penmanship gave you away," she said. "Your writing on the labels that we're sorting Creelman's books by matches the writing used for the secret codes in the mystery novels."

"Very clever," Loyola said.

"Also," she continued, "we discovered you in a yearbook photograph of the Queensview Mystery Book Club. You, Trevor and Mr. Easton."

Loyola nodded along.

"And I'm guessing that it was Mr. Easton who wrote you the note you've got pinned to your bulletin board. In fact — " Merrilee held up the paper to have a closer look at the writing on Loyola's essay cover — "I'm sure this is the same handwriting as in the book we found in Trevor Tower's locker. *Tell the Club that Buster's doing fine.* Same loopy backward-slanted penmanship. Was Mr. Easton left-handed?"

My stomach gave a guilty lurch at the mention of Murray Easton's book, which was actually still lying on my night table, *not* in Trevor's locker.

"He was," Loyola confirmed.

"And there's one more thing I'm sure of," Merrilee declared. "It was you who put Murray Easton's book inside Trevor Tower's time capsule. You probably put all those letters written to him in there, too."

"No," Loyola said, shaking her head. "You're wrong about the letters."

Merrilee stepped back and crossed her arms.

Pascal and I still stood behind Merrilee, taking it all in.

Loyola took the prized paper from Merrilee and folded it to pin to her bulletin board. When she turned back to face us, she sighed.

"Okay," she said. "Time to explain."

"Start with the Queensview Mystery Book Club," Merrilee demanded, uncrossing her arms.

"That's a good place to start," Loyola agreed, clearing her throat. "As I told you, Mr. Easton was the best teacher I ever had. He came to Queensview Elementary when I started grade six, just the age you are now."

"Why was he so great?" Merrilee asked.

"I don't know," Loyola said. "Maybe it was how he

held so many of his classes outside. Maybe it was how he got us to really think about novels. Maybe it was the famous authors and interesting guest speakers he brought in to read to us. Maybe it was how he made writing fun and exciting. We were so proud to share our work out loud with each other. I guess it was all of those things."

Loyola was describing the teacher I had already met in Murray Easton's book.

"And he started a mystery book club?" Merrilee asked.

"Yes, he did. I can't tell you the number of books we all read and discussed, but it was a lot."

"Trevor Tower was a member," Merrilee said.

"That's right. And here's where it gets interesting. For our community service duty, Trevor and I served on the Senior Citizens' Pet Patrol."

"The what?" Merrilee asked.

"The Senior Citizens' Pet Patrol. We were able to sign up with the animal shelter. The shelter used to have a program where volunteers helped senior citizens by walking their dogs."

"What does this have to do with Trevor Tower's time capsule?" Merrilee asked.

"I'm getting to that," Loyola said. "Every Wednesday, we used to pick up the dogs from the seniors in the program, and Trevor and I would walk their dogs in the park. But one of the seniors who signed up lived alone and had no dog. He claimed that he had lost his dog and that he wanted us to keep a lookout for it."

"A lost dog?" Merrilee repeated.

"Yes. A lost dog with spots."

I sucked in my breath. A spotted dog? There it was again! The name of Murray Easton's novel. The epitaph in the book Creelman loaned me. *And now this!*

"Did you help him look for the dog?" I jumped in and asked.

"At first we did. But then we thought that maybe he was a bit senile. We thought he was making things up. And then one day when we dropped by the animal shelter, we learned that his son had moved him away to live nearer to the son's family."

Loyola paused. She took a sip from her water bottle.

"Go on," Merrilee prodded.

"Later, Trevor saw it. A spotted dog. He rushed into the school to tell me. I ran outside with him to check it out."

"Where was it?" I asked.

"Trevor said that he had last seen it by the school fence. So that's where we headed."

The Spotted Dog Last Seen, I silently repeated. *The Spotted Dog Last Seen*.

"And then?" Merrilee asked.

"We both saw it. A scruffy little thing with spots on its legs and face. And it sunk in. The senior citizen had been telling us the truth all along."

"Did you track down the senior citizen? Tell him you saw his dog?" I asked.

"Yes, but he couldn't take the dog where he was living. No dogs allowed. So he begged us to find the dog a new home."

Loyola paused for another sip of water.

"The spotted dog was hard to catch. Eventually, it started hanging around the outdoor classes that Mr. Easton held."

I shivered. It felt like I was back in the cemetery on that first day, waiting in the rain for the Brigade to arrive.

Loyola continued.

"It was about then that Mr. Easton decided to move back to Ferndale, to teach in his hometown. We were very sad. And Trevor, who had been assigned a time capsule at the end of grade six, offered to donate the space to the Queensview Mystery Book Club so that members could deposit their final projects for Mr. Easton inside."

"What happened to the spotted dog?" I asked.

"Mr. Creelman finally caught it. And Mr. Easton adopted the dog to take back with him to Ferndale."

I stopped to think. What had Murray Easton written by hand in his book?

Tell the Club that Buster's doing fine!

Buster, the spotted dog!

"Well, at least that part worked out," I said.

"It did in the end," Loyola said. "Apparently, the dog was a handful. The senior citizen who owned the dog told us that he would read to it. He said that was the only way to calm the dog down."

"Movie scripts," I blurted without thinking.

Loyola looked up at me, eyebrows raised.

"That's right. He'd read movie scripts to the dog for hours on end. Mr. Easton had to do that, too."

"But *The Spotted Dog Last Seen* was published a year later. How did that novel get into the locker?" Merrilee asked.

"I ran into Mr. Easton at a book signing. He gave me a copy, which I read, and that gave me the idea to start a mystery book club of my own. I remembered Trevor's locker combination, so I added the book."

"That's when you started donating books anonymously and writing secret codes in them," Merrilee said.

Loyola nodded. "I've been doing it every year ever since. Quite a few students have now solved the codes," she said proudly. "And read plenty of mystery books in the process as they found their way to Trevor's locker."

"Why'd you pick me?" Merrilee asked.

"Simple. You signed out a book about secret codes for your book report earlier this year, remember? That made you a good candidate."

"Okay, so you get students to read a bunch of novels just like the Queensview Mystery Book Club, and that leads them to Trevor Tower's locker, which contains Mr. Easton's novel. Now, what about the pile of letters inside? Were those the last assignments?"

Good question, I thought. That stack of sealed letters in the locker all written to Mr. Easton. What could they be about?

"Not all of them. Just the earliest ones in the pile. Those ones are on the bottom."

"Just the ones on the bottom? So the other letters must have been written by those who discovered the locker before us."

"Correct," Loyola said.

"Why would they write letters for a time capsule?" Merrilee asked.

"Why?" Loyola asked incredulously. "You haven't read Mr. Easton's book? *The Spotted Dog Last Seen*?"

"No," Merrilee said, removing her glasses and cleaning the lenses with her shirttail. "Not yet."

Loyola turned to me.

I gulped. I was about to be caught red-handed. I should not have blurted out, "Movie scripts."

She knew I knew.

I took the tiniest step back. Loyola started to say something to me, but then returned her attention to Merrilee.

"You need to read the book," Loyola said. She looked at Pascal and me. "All of you. It explains the last assignment. It explains *everything*."

I thought back to the book on my night table. I was about three-quarters of the way through, and it was not explaining *anything* as far as I could see. Sure, it was about a teacher who was obviously based on Mr. Easton, who liked to teach outdoors, who had a crazy spotted dog that liked to be read to.

Unless ...

Unless something huge happened in the last few chapters. Something that would link everything together, tie everything up perfectly the way mystery novels always do.

I needed to get back to that book. I needed to finish reading it, even if it kept me up all night.

Loyola reached underneath her counter and laid three library copies of *The Spotted Dog Last Seen* on top.

"I thought all the copies were signed out," Merrilee accused.

"They are. In your names," Loyola said with a smile. "I've been expecting you."

It was too much for me.

"Whoa. Look at the time," I said, pointing at the wall clock above the book returns.

I grabbed my copy and got out of there as fast as I could.

But not before rescuing Creelman's book from the recycling table, the one with the crayon marks and the missing pages. I stuffed both books into my knapsack.

That night, right after dinner, I holed up in my bedroom and returned to the time capsule's copy of *The Spotted Dog Last Seen*. It was hard to concentrate. I kept thinking that a major incident was going to leap out at me with every page turn. Nothing did.

And then, when it was quite late — eight minutes after midnight — I got to the chapter that nearly made me fall off my bed. I went to get a glass of water from the bathroom, then returned to my room and read the chapter all over again, slowly this time, so that I could memorize every detail.

Chapter 11.

In it, the teacher thinks back to a school where he had previously taught. It was in a nearby town. He misses that town and the students in that school very much, but he can never return. He goes on to explain why.

His recollection starts happily enough. He was going on a date. He had met her at the school where they both worked. She was teaching the grade fours. He was teaching the grade threes. They had lunch together in the teachers' room every day for months and months, an entire school year, in fact. But when school was finally dismissed for the summer, he still had not proved brave enough to ask her out.

Then it was July, and the weather was hot and sticky. He went for an ice cream cone at the town's only dairy bar and ran into her in the long lineup.

"What a scorcher," he said, making small talk, his heart thumping madly.

"I'll say," she said. "I spent forever in the frozen aisle of the grocery store today."

"I'm thinking of going to the movies tonight," said the teacher, playing along, "just for the air conditioning."

"Great idea! Can I come with you?" she asked.

"Oh," said the teacher.

"Oh?" she repeated with a smile.

"Yes," said the teacher, recovering. "I can pick you up. What's a good time?"

"Eight," she said. She wrote her address down on a napkin that had her lipstick smudge on the corner. "See you then."

The teacher could hardly think for the rest of the day. He busied himself by cleaning his apartment, despite the sticky heat, and he wrote another poem to add to his collection of the ones he had already written about her. He even toyed with the idea of bringing some of his poetry to read to her on their first date, but then thought no, too soon.

He tried on four different pairs of pants and seven shirts before he settled on what to wear. He tried to fix his thick wavy hair, but it would not cooperate. It never did. He brushed his teeth. Twice. Then he got into his car with the broken air conditioner, rolled down all the windows, hoping she wouldn't notice, and drove out to the neighborhood where she lived.

He was not familiar with her neighborhood. It was

new, with young trees and no shade, and all the houses looked the same. He got lost a few times, and when he finally found her street, he was terribly late. Nearly frantic, he anxiously scanned each house for its street address before scooting past to the next one.

The heat was unbearable in the car, even with all the windows down. Everyone who lived on the street was inside.

Not everyone.

While looking out the side window for the next house address, he felt a sickening thud on the hood of his car. He automatically hit the brakes. The teacher peered through the windshield. A little boy flew into the air, reaching out to him. The little boy landed near the curb. The little boy did not move again.

The teacher flung his door open and rushed to the little boy. The buzzing sound of a nearby lawnmower stopped. Screen doors creaked open up and down the street like question marks. The teacher knelt beside the little boy. He was dead. The teacher yelled for help anyway.

A crowd gathered and several people pushed him out of the way to attend to the little boy. Others shouted, "Call 911!"

The teacher staggered backwards, away from the crowd, away from the body of the little boy, and he collapsed on a lawn with his head in his hands.

Why? Why?

Why did that little boy run in front of his car?

He briefly looked up. Across the street, jammed under a parked car, was an orange rubber ball.

And beside him, standing alone, not with the crowd, was another little boy about the same age, stiff and motionless, staring at the teacher. That other little boy hardly blinked, his arms hung at his sides. He said nothing. He was so pale, like a ghost. And then that boy's mother rushed to him, scooped up her small son and carried him inside their house.

"Derek?"

I looked up from my bed. My mom stood at my bedroom door.

"What are you still doing up? You have school tomorrow."

"I'm almost done my book," I said. "Just a few more pages."

She hesitated.

"Is everything okay?"

I looked at her, but who I saw was a younger version of my mom, my mom who had hugged me so hard after the accident that I thought she'd never let me go.

"Just a few more pages," I assured her.

She closed my door. I went back to where I had left off. The last chapter.

After the police investigation, which ruled the little

boy's death an accident, the teacher could not get past his grief. He had trouble leaving his apartment, he ate very little, and he cried several times a day. Letters and bills piled up, and the thought of going back to his old school in the fall to teach made him feel sick to his stomach.

Finally, someone from his school board paid him a visit. After he reluctantly agreed to let her in, he told her he was stuck. He could not move forward. He could not get past the accident. He could barely leave his apartment with all the curtains drawn shut.

She handed him a letter of transfer, which meant he could move to a nearby town, teach at a new school and start over where no one knew about the accident.

After she left, the teacher sat at his kitchen table for a very long time. He struggled to remember what it felt like to be in front of a classroom. He started to remember fleeting bits and pieces. A couple of times, he remembered moments of joy. The questions students asked with their hands up. The smell of new books. The school buzzer calling everyone in from recess.

He got up and made himself a sandwich. He opened his living-room curtains and stood at the window while he chewed. He realized that he loved teaching, and he was good at it.

The teacher signed the letter of transfer. And then, while he was settling in his new town, while he got to know his new students and while he made room for a lost spotted dog who loved movie scripts, he wrote it all down.

I looked at the clock on my night table. It was 1:14 a.m. I put *The Spotted Dog Last Seen* into my knapsack and pulled out Creelman's book about rockets. I studied the crayon marks on the cover and the uneven scissor cuts inside.

The work of a four-year-old. The work of Dennis.

I slid that book beside my treasured journal of t-shirt sayings on the bookshelf above my desk. Then I crawled back into bed and turned out the light. I lay there, piecing together everything I knew.

Dennis.

Mr. Creelman.

Murray Easton.

Loyola Louden.

The mystery novel code.

Trevor Tower's time capsule.

The Spotted Dog Last Seen.

The pile of letters.

I knew then what was in those letters. The first ones were by Mr. Easton's former students. Just like Murray Easton, they had written about their own tragedies, their own sadness, their own disappointments as a way to get unstuck, as a way to move forward. The later ones, the ones on top of the pile, were from others who had discovered the locker before us and who had also read *The Spotted Dog Last Seen*. Having found a safe place for their own painful stories, they had kept Mr. Easton's assignment going.

Trevor Tower did keep secrets after all.

When I woke up in the morning, something was different. I should have been tired from the late night, but I wasn't. In fact, I had slept well.

"Where's Dad?" I asked at breakfast.

"He had to leave early for a meeting," my mom said, pouring milk on my cereal. "Did you finish your book?"

"Yes," I said, and took a couple of crunchy mouthfuls. "Mom, can I ask you something?"

"Sure you can," she said, sitting down with her coffee and toast.

"It's about Dennis," I said.

She froze.

"Is this about your nightmares?"

"Actually, I didn't have one last night. But I'm curious. Do you remember anything about the driver who hit him?"

My mom set down her piece of toast with only one bite gone.

"I don't remember seeing him at the time of the accident. I brought you inside as soon as I found you on the lawn. You were in shock."

"So, you don't know who the driver was?"

She thought some more.

"I remember that there was a police investigation. The driver was found to be not at fault. The police decided that Dennis's death was an accident. It was in the newspaper."

"There was an article in the newspaper?" I asked.

"I have the article," she said quietly, studying my face.

"You do?"

"Yes. Our family doctor back in Ferndale told me to keep it, in case you wanted to know more when you got older."

"Can I see it now?" I asked, trying very hard to steady my voice so as not to alarm her.

"Okay," she said.

She stood and went upstairs. I could hear her open a closet door, followed by some rummaging sounds.

My thoughts turned frantic. What if she had lost the article after all these years? Having finally come so close to the truth about that terrible day, would it now slip away forever?

"Here," she said, handing me a yellowed newspaper clipping, its yellowness reminding me of Creelman's notes on our first day of cemetery duty.

I studied the photograph at the top of the article. It was Murray Easton, head down, leaving Ferndale's law court building. He was all alone. The caption below read, "Child's death by local teacher ruled accidental."

Twelve

Ferndale

WHEN I GOT TO school that Thursday, I waited on the front steps for Pascal and Merrilee. Pascal was the first to arrive.

"Wait with me for Merrilee," I said. "I've got something to tell you both."

"Something about our case?" he asked eagerly.

"You could say that," I said, my knapsack weighing heavily at my feet. My head was swirling with the truth.

"What's up?" Merrilee said when she arrived moments later.

I led them inside the school to a quiet part of the hallway where a table with year end lost-and-found items were on display: scarves from last winter, one rubber boot, calculators, skipping ropes, a mountain of school uniform parts and a harmonica.

"Oh, that's where it went," Merrilee said, pocketing

the harmonica. "I thought I'd lost it the last time I practiced at the cemetery."

She turned her attention to me as if she'd said nothing peculiar at all.

"I read the book," I confessed. "*The Spotted Dog Last Seen*."

"Already?" Merrilee and Pascal asked at the same time.

"Yes. The whole thing."

"How did you read it so quickly?" Merrilee asked incredulously.

"I took the copy from the locker right after we broke in. I've been reading it ever since."

Merrilee's jaw dropped.

"So much for teamwork," Pascal muttered.

"Loyola was right," I said, ignoring Pascal. "You'll both need to read Murray Easton's book over the weekend if you want to complete the last assignment before the school closes on Monday."

"Complete the last assignment?" Pascal repeated. "Sounds like work! And school's almost over. You said it yourself."

"You'll see. You'll want to complete the last assignment like the others," I insisted.

Merrilee and Pascal just stood there.

Like Wooster and Preeble.

Perhaps it was my sober no-nonsense tone that confused them. I must have sounded like Creelman.

I turned and walked away.

That weekend, my mom and I drove to Ferndale. My dad stayed home, inspired by the spring weather to clean up his workshop. He waved to us from his wide-open garage door, then turned to face the contents.

"Good grief!" I heard him say as we got into the car.

On the way there, my mom made small talk.

"I can't believe you're almost done grade six," she said.

"It's no big deal," I replied, staring out the side window, a canvas bag of art supplies at my feet.

"It *is* a big deal. You'll be leaving Queensview Elementary behind. You'll be saying goodbye to all your old teachers. You'll be going to a brand-new school — junior high! — and meeting new friends this fall. You're growing up so fast."

Her voice got all choky as she gripped the steering wheel.

I looked down at my t-shirt. It read, *Every great achievement was once thought impossible.*

"We had the time-capsule ceremony on Friday," I said to lighten the mood.

"Whose locker was chosen?"

"Marcus Papadopoulos."

"What did he put in?"

"The usual stuff. His gym socks, which I don't think he washed the entire year. An Egyptian pharaoh mask

THE SPOTTED DOG LAST SEEN | 193

he made in art class. His dad's old toy model of the Batmobile. His sex education book. And an empty ant farm he made for the science fair."

"When will his time capsule be reopened?" she asked.

"Fifty years," I said.

My mom whistled.

"That's a long time," she said.

"I'll be old by then," I added.

"I certainly hope so," she said, almost to herself.

We drove in silence as we entered Ferndale. When she pulled up to the cemetery gate and parked the car, she turned to me.

"Are you sure about this?"

I paused. Only a few months ago, cemeteries gave me the creeps. But I had come to understand the special kind of silence that surrounded them. It was a silence created by countless untold stories, and it blanketed the gravestones like a homemade patchwork quilt.

"Yes," I said, grabbing my bag of art supplies. "You called and got permission, right?"

"I did," she said, putting the car keys in her purse.

Ferndale's Bellevue Cemetery was much like Twillingate. It was surrounded by a black iron fence with a large swinging gate that was locked up with chains at night. We wandered through the oldest section nearest to the gate. It was crammed with teetering gravestones made of slate or sandstone mixed in with the wolf stones, marbles and obelisks in the middle distance. We even passed some white wooden crosses poking up from the lumpy ground.

Everything faced west.

The inscriptions were eroding.

But the sky was surprisingly blue.

If it had been any other day, if we had not been on a mission, I would have pointed out some things to my mom. Like what the skulls and crossbones really meant. Like how different types of stone weathered at different rates. Like how to tell an eroded number 1 from a number 4 by using a simple mirror trick.

Instead, we worked our way past the old-timers into the newest section of the cemetery, where granite blocks stood perfectly upright and gleamed in the spring-almost-summer sunshine.

There were so many.

So many.

"Do you remember where?" I asked.

My mom stopped and looked around uncertainly.

"I'm not sure. It was such a sad day."

"I remember a stone lamb," I said.

She stared at me.

"That's right. A lamb. An innocent lamb. I remember that, too."

So we picked our way up and down the rows in search of Dennis's lamb.

Up and down.

Up and down.

Up and down.

"Derek," my mom called.

I caught up to her.

We stood in front of Dennis's gravestone.

Such a small thing. Just his name. The short time between his date of birth and his death. And the words deeply etched in stone beneath the dates that read, *How much sorrow, how much joy is buried with our darling boy*.

I walked up to the carved stone lamb that was resting on top of Dennis's gravestone, its head turned slightly toward passersby. I placed my hand on its little head and was surprised to feel its warmth.

I reached into my bag and pulled out Creelman's book of epitaphs, *Famous Last Words*, along with my note to Dennis's mom tucked between the covers. My note read, *I will always remember your son and your father. Sincerely, Derek Knowles-Collier*.

I had placed the book in a plastic bag with a sealed top, for protection from the weather. I was about to lay it at the base of Dennis's gravestone, when I discovered a small toy rocket leaning against the back of the stone. There was a tag tied to it with a ribbon. I bent down to read the tag.

Your grandfather faltered by the wayside, and the angels took him home. Now he can teach you all about the twinkly stars.

"What does it say?" my mom asked.

But there was no way I could read *those* words out loud. My throat was squeezed too tight. Instead, I shook my head, laid Creelman's book at the base and handed her the toy. Then I busied myself by digging out my art supplies.

I followed Creelman's instructions perfectly. I made a beautiful rubbing of Dennis's epitaph while my mom sat on the grass and quietly watched, cradling the little rocket on her lap.

When I was done, I carefully folded the rubbing into a square and packed up my supplies.

We put the little rocket back where we found it, next to Creelman's book.

"All set?" my mom asked, her arm around my shoulders.

But I knew what she really meant.

"I'm okay," I said, and I gave her an extra long hug to prove it.

It was late when we got home, having stopped along the way for supper. Tomorrow was the last day of school, only a half day, really, because we would be let out at noon. But I still had a few things to do before I went to bed.

Back in my room, I found a large envelope and slid the folded rubbing of Dennis's gravestone inside. Then I added the yellowed newspaper article about Murray

Easton, all according to my plan. But there was something missing. I lay down on my bed to think.

Dennis's death was not my fault. I knew that now with undeniable relief. I also knew that it wasn't Murray Easton's fault. And it wasn't Dennis's fault, either. So I wanted to add something to the envelope that would free us all from that terrible day.

Some kindly act.

Some words of comfort.

Something.

But what?

That night, I had the nightmare one last time. It started the exact same way as it always did.

I am sitting on the front steps eating a popsicle, checking out a scab on my knee. The cement is warm beneath me. I can smell the fresh grass. The lawn has just been cut, and my dad rolls his mower to the backyard. A screen door squeaks, and it's my friend, Dennis, from the brick house beside us. I wave. He's holding an orange rubber ball.

Dennis cuts across the newly mown grass. He kicks the ball to me. I try to kick it back, but I miss. He laughs. I laugh, too, as I scramble to get the ball. I kick it to him. He misses. We laugh.

The sun is warm.

The grass is sweet.

The orange ball is tricky.

We are the only ones playing outside on our little street, with the young trees just planted and the houses brand-new. It is too hot for most people, and there is no shade. They stay indoors where it is cool. My mom is on the couch with a headache, a bag of ice around her neck. We are the only ones outside, except for my dad, who is cutting the lawn in the backyard, and Murray Easton, who is driving his car with all the windows down along our street, searching for an address.

I miss again. The ball rolls under a bush by our front steps. When I crawl over to get it, I bump the scab on my knee and it starts bleeding. When I stand, bits of freshly cut grass are sticking to my legs.

It is so hot out. There is no shade. The sun is coming down, and it is right in my face whenever I look over to where Dennis is. I cannot see him because of the sun, but I hear him laughing.

I put the orange rubber ball down in front of me. I stand back. Then I take a run at the ball and kick it as hard as I can.

Bam! Perfect hit. It soars over my lawn and Dennis's lawn, too. It soars over the sidewalk. It soars onto the street.

I look for Dennis, but the sun is still in the way. Dennis turns to chase the ball, and now the sun is in his way. And because of the lawnmower, he does not hear the car. Murray Easton's car.

Dennis runs.

Brakes squeal.

Dennis flies backwards into the air, his arms reaching out to the driver who has just hit him, his legs dangling. He crumples to the ground.

I hear sounds of a car door opening.

Murray Easton yells for help.

The lawnmower stops.

Screen doors creak open along both sides of my street.

I make myself walk to the curb. My legs do not work well.

Dennis is lying on the road. His eyes are open, but he is not moving.

His head is in a puddle of blood. The puddle is spreading.

Someone pushes me aside as she rushes by.

Dennis's mom.

Then my dad.

Now a crowd surrounds Dennis.

Murray Easton collapses onto our lawn. He groans as he rocks back and forth, his head in his hands.

I hear sirens.

Someone puts his hand on my shoulder. I turn to look.

It is you.

You say to me, "All seats have an equal view of the universe."

I can hear you perfectly. I nod. I understand.

Then you walk over to Murray Easton who is still on the lawn, rocking, rocking.

"All seats have an equal view of the universe,"
you say to him. You hold out your hand and help Murray Easton slowly to his feet.

I woke up with a sense of total calm. It was still dark outside, but just before dawn. I found a blank t-shirt in my cupboard and started cutting out letters from my iron-on stencil kit. I grabbed my mom's iron from the laundry room and heated it up. I laid a towel on the floor, then the t-shirt with the arranged letters, and I ironed the letters. I held up the t-shirt to admire my work.

All seats have an equal view of the universe.

I put it on and slipped outside. The sun was not yet up, but the stars were softly fading. I lay down on my back, eyes closed. I could smell the grass as I listened through the silence for the untold stories above me. I listened until I could hear laughter. Just laughter. Dennis's laughter.

Back upstairs, I took off the t-shirt and folded it. I tucked the t-shirt into the envelope along with the gravestone rubbing and the newspaper article. Then I sealed the envelope and wrote the name *Mr. Easton* in my best penmanship.

The sun had started to rise.

I did not come across Merrilee or Pascal on my last day of school. Merrilee skipped the day so that she could go to the airport to meet her grandmother who was visiting for the summer from Japan.

And Pascal? I'm not sure where he was. But he left a note on my locker. It read, *Here's a t-shirt saying for you — Zombies eat brains. You're safe.* And then, in smaller letters, he wrote, *My birthday's in a few weeks. Pool party. Hope you can make it.*

I lingered in the hallway well after the last student charged out the front doors at the noon-hour bell. Even the teachers didn't seem to be around.

After I cleaned out my own locker and stuffed everything into my knapsack, I looked one last time at the empty space inside, the space that had held so much of my life this past year, the space now filled with dead air. I could feel sadness edging toward me, so I quickly turned away and headed upstairs, leaving the door ajar for someone new to fill the locker.

Some of the classroom windows had been left open, and I felt a soft breeze on the back of my neck as I stood in front of Trevor Tower's locker.

Twenty-eight. Thirty-four. Eighteen.

When I opened the locker, I returned Murray Easton's book to the shelf, exactly as we had found it. I picked up two new envelopes at the top of the stack on the floor of the locker. Both were addressed to Mr. Easton. I recognized Pascal's and Merrilee's penmanship. But their envelopes were sealed like all the others beneath, each one containing its own secret.

Then, on a hunch, I pulled out the envelope at the very bottom of the stack. It, too, was addressed to Mr. Easton, but in Loyola Louden's handwriting with the hooded *a*. I wondered if she had written about not believing the senior citizen who had lost his spotted dog. And if so, I wondered if she had been able to forgive herself for doubting the elderly man's story.

I like to think that she had.

I put the envelopes back the way they were, then laid my own envelope on top of the pile. I closed the door and spun the dial, an act so final, I knew I would never be back.

But even as I walked outside and down the vacant steps toward the cemetery to visit the granites lined up with precision, I knew that Trevor Tower's time capsule, the keeper of secrets, had endless patience. Like the past, the locker I had just locked would not stay locked for long.

A locker unlocked.

Untold stories told.

The buried remembered.

Again.

And again.

Acknowledgments

I AM INDEBTED to many people who helped me during this project, or inspired me in some way or another that worked its way into the details.

Thank you, Maura Gair, instructor at Fountain Academy of the Sacred Heart School in Halifax. You taught the boys about the importance of community service. Having watched the news story about the students working in my neighborhood cemetery during which you and Sean Mullally were interviewed, I was inspired to detour into Halifax's Old Burying Ground on my way home from work. There I came across a slate double marker with an epitaph on only one side, and I was inspired to fill in the blank by writing this novel.

Thank you, Bill Druker and D.J. DeCoste. Murray Easton is meant to showcase the exceptional teaching qualities you both demonstrate as faculty members of Fountain Academy.

Thank you, Nancy Zinck. You were an especially enthusiastic writing student of mine. You faithfully recorded my lectures, bought all my early books and had me sign them to send to your relatives out west, and then during the last class, presented me with a homemade knitted red scarf. I learned through my writer's association newsletter that you died shortly after. Merrilee's charming red plastic jacket with the bunnies-and-carrots pattern is in memory of you.

Thank you, Access Copyright Foundation. You supported my research by contributing to the costs of attending the annual conference of the Association of Gravestone Studies in New Jersey, where I presented my work to a large room of mostly archaeologists. There I secured a number of readers for this manuscript as well as learned about the fine art of cemetery care.

Thank you to my manuscript readers: Siobhan Lavelle and your nephew, David Lavelle, Judith Trainor, Cheryle Caputo, Kathleen Mannino, Gwen Enos, Susan Acampora, Louis deSalle, Sandhya Srivastava, Jack Wooldridge and Trevor Fowler (who also keeps me supplied with interesting names). You all provided helpful feedback, and I tried to make the changes you suggested. If there are any additional errors, they are my own.

Thank you, Judith Trainor, for making space for me in your over-enrolled workshop on how to make a foil impression of a gravestone carving. You patiently encouraged me to finish my first attempt — an angel kneeling beside an anchor, the symbol of hope — despite all the foil wrinkles I couldn't smooth out. Derek chooses this symbol for his own gravestone in chapter 7.

Thank you, Debra McNabb. I plucked *a tapestry of sighs* from one of many elegantly written emails I received from you in which you reflect on some heritage-related issue. Inspired by that phrase, I wrote my epitaph to the fire-station mascot in chapter 9.

Thank you, Bill Greenlaw and David Ross. You've shown kind interest in my writing during moments between the pressing issues of the day. Also, thank you to Kevin Barrett and Laura Bennett, two dedicated heritage specialists who work to protect my province's cemeteries, even the abandoned ones. You both have all kinds of stories to tell.

Thank you, Rhonda Walker, for pulling over so that I could stomp around particularly interesting cemeteries with my camera. You wouldn't get out of the car, but still. You continue to indulge my efforts to better understand whatever subject matter is at hand.

Thank you, Elliott Kerrin. You renewed my fascination with stars and planetariums when you shared your astronomy notes and photographs from Queen's University with me. Creelman's career as a planetarium projectionist is a nod to our conversations. And even though we now live in separate provinces, I'm comforted that we still share an equal view of the universe.

Thank you, Peter Kerrin. You're like Derek's dad in several ways — your sporting good nature that allows you to don a t-shirt with a slogan that Elliott made up and proudly wear it to the gym; the organizational approach you apply to your workshop in the basement, which is crammed with home projects in various states; and your love of peanut butter and jam sandwiches. You're a great dad.

And thank you, thank you, Sheila Barry. When I was feeling lost and searching for a publisher, you offered a home for this book along with your expert editorial support. In that regard, I am the spotted dog.

About the Author

JESSICA SCOTT KERRIN is the author of the newly launched Lobster Chronicles trilogy and the bestselling Martin Bridge series. *Martin Bridge: Ready for Takeoff* was chosen by the *Horn Book* and the New York Public Library as one of the best books of 2005.

Born and raised in Alberta, Jessica moved to Nova Scotia to study at the Nova Scotia College of Art and Design. Surrounded by shipyards, fog and historic cemeteries, she remains in downtown Halifax, where she lives with her family and pet tortoise, and continues to build her writing career.